# BROTHERS OF THE WIND
## *The Saga Of An Angloromani Family*

by

Thomas Bryer

**Grey Forest Press**

# BROTHERS OF THE WIND

Copyright © Thomas Bryer 2018
Greyforest Press, LLC
Oak Harbor, Ohio
ISBN 9780983258322
LCCN 2018907125
info@greyforestpress.com

*"There's the wind on the heath brother, if I could only feel that, I would gladly live forever."*
George Borrow
*Lavengro*

# Prologue

The life of a Gypsy has always been filled with stark contrasts, with love or hate, with grief or joy, and with feast or famine. The Gypsies' existence has faithfully followed this up and down cycle ever since their earliest mention in the annals of England.

In the sixteenth century, laws were enacted that made merely being a Gypsy, or impersonating one, a capital offense. The Gypsies enjoyed brief periods of peace and prosperity after these edicts were canceled. But in the early 1800s, life became a struggle once more for the English Gypsies. The new Industrial Revolution wielded a double-edged sword against the Gypsies' way of life. Mass production of cheap household goods made it difficult for the Gypsies to earn a living by manufacturing and peddling their rustic brooms, clothes pegs, and baskets. Rapid industrialization brought with it an explosion in population. Land enclosure Acts and the farmers were putting every available piece of land to the plow. Their old camping sites were rapidly disappearing, and stiff new laws against vagrancy made it difficult for the Gypsies to find a place to rest. Seldom could a family camp beside a lane without having a constable come along and drive them off.

One of the last refuges in the south of England for the Gypsies was the great New Forest. Of all the forests in England around 1830, the great New Forest still retained more of the character of a medieval woodland. Covering nearly thirty miles square, from across the Solent on its southern boundary lay the Isle of Wight, to the east is Southampton Water. The plains of Salisbury encroach to the north and the river Avon forms its western boundary.

The forest was interspersed with hamlets and farms and forest huts. All manner of man dwelt in the confines of New Forest: preachers and poachers, smugglers, Lords and charcoal burners, Gypsies and small holders. Small holders were the squatters who had earned the right to live in the forest and let their branded livestock roam its confines.

Upper class sportsmen and local gentry were still covetous of the forest game, just as in the early days of the forest when it was established as a royal hunting park. For that reason, every major forest had wardens and keepers who posted areas and levied stiff fines and imprisonment upon the common man who dared to hunt or trap wild game. No man felt the weight of these laws more than the Gypsy, for the forest was his larder and the heath his garden.

The Gypsy would pitch his tent in the forest some distance from the town where his family would hopefully be at peace while he produced from the raw materials of the forest his rustic household goods, clothes pegs and willow baskets. His women would sell these in the villages or trade them to farm wives for produce, butter or poultry.

England

# CHAPTER 1

It was autumn in the great New Forest, a quiet time when the forest birds had ceased to sing and the glowing purple carpets of heather spread over the moorlands that intersperse the heaths and thickets of this primeval place.

English Gypsy Adam Stanley was in his early thirties, he was a tall man by any ones standards. He had a well-formed and muscular body and his jet black hair curled behind his ears beneath a fine felt hat. His trousers were of lambskin and he wore a green waistcoat with a row of silver coin buttons running down each side of the front.

Adam's normally smiling face had a troubled expression this day as he slowly steered his wagon off of the narrow rutted lane. He stepped down from his wagon and leaned in to pick up his sleeping five-year-old son Tom from his wife Vashti's arms. The child's bright, red face and vacant eyes exposed the fact that he was very ill with a fever. Adam carried the small bundle of warmth over to a nearby spring and sat him down gently. He lovingly washed the child's face with a wet cloth then he dipped a handful of cool clear water and held it up to his lips. The child sucked the water in then in a frail hoarse voice he asked, "More Daddy, more."

Vashti, now by Adam's side took the child from him. She picked him up and held her face to his, "He's still burning up, Adam. We should never have taken this *chavy* (child) to the Downs. There were so many sick people there. I pray that it's not the pox."

"I doubt it is the pox, dear."

"Adam, There was an old poxy *mumper*(beggar) there, died in his tent out behind the stalls. His family just took him behind a hedge and covered him with brush whilst they went on drinking and begging. I sure hope that our Tom didn't get around any of their filthy chavies."

"I'm sure that it's not the pox. When I took our boys last year to visit Uncle Sylvester, he had his friend, the surgeon at Stoney Cross, dose us with cowpox as a prevention. He assured us that from then on we would be safe from catching the bad pox. I didn't tell you because I knew how you felt about such things."

"Adam, so when you brought the boys back, that's why they had those sores on their little arms and they was sick with a bit of fever. How could you do that without asking me?"

"If I would have asked you, you would have said no and I wanted to do something to protect them. Too many of our people have been taken away from us by the pox, so I had to give our boys a chance."

Vashti knew that when it came to this deadly scourge, her own knowledge of Gypsy herbal remedies were useless. "I won't fault you, my husband, I know that what you did was only for our boy's sake, but do you think we should keep going and get our Tom to the doctor?"

"No, we will stay here for the night and do what we can for him."

Adam walked over and grabbed his horse's reins. He guided it and the wagon up an overgrown path into a small clearing away from the lane. He unhooked his horse and tied it out on a patch of grass, then he proceeded to set up his small bender tent. He took an iron rod (his pot crane) and he poked six uniform holes in the ground. In these holes, he placed three semicircular bent rods made of ash wood. These formed the hoop frame for his tent. He covered this frame with heavy waterproof felt blankets which he secured with sharp wooden pins. Adam filled the floor of the tent with straw from his wagon, then he placed a blanket over the straw. Vashti had already gathered some dry wood and, she soon had a crackling fire after working the steel and flint. She took an iron pot and carried it to the nearby spring.

Any other time she would have taken her leisure and enjoyed her lovely surroundings, but now her mind was troubled. She only had time to fill her pot with water and grab a handful of bright green watercress, which was growing at the edge of a small pool below the spring. She knew that Adam always loved to chew a bit of watercress with his meal, especially his favorite hare stew.

Vashti took the pot and placed it on a pot crane over the smokey, crackling fire, leaving it to boil. She then grabbed a knife and struck out again into the forest. Vashti finally came upon a young willow while glancing from tree to tree. She located some smooth, green bark and stripped off enough bark to fill the large pouch in her apron.

With quick steps, Vashti hurried back to the camp

and her sick child. "How is my Tom?" She asked, leaning down and looking into the opening in the tent.

"He's not any better." Adam answered, as he sat cross legged on the blanket, cradling the sick child in his arms. Vashti was even more concerned now. She took the peelings of willow bark from her apron and placed them in the pot of now simmering water. She carefully weighted down the bark with the end on a long handled silver spoon, making sure that all of the bark became submerged. Soon the water took on a greenish tint and the steam carried the woody essence of willow bark up into Vashti's nostrils. She knew now that her concoction was ready. She filled a tin cup from the pot and set it aside to cool.

Several minutes passed, Vashti cautiously placed her finger into the greenish liquid and, having found that it was cool enough to drink, she carried it to little Tommy. She brought the cup up to little Tom's lips. He caught a smell of the concoction and grimaced, "It smells bad, mother."

"If you drink it, my baby, then I will buy you a bag of sweet treats when we get to town."

Tom's eyes narrowed and flickered as he steeled himself. He began to drink from the cup. He gagged and coughed, "Was I good, Mother? Will I get them treats tomorrow?"

"Sure you will, my baby. Now you lay down and let the medicine do its work while your mother gets something ready for us to eat."

Vashti went to the wagon, reaching into a burlap bag. She removed several large potatoes. She took a stick and dug into the campfire ashes to create a small pit into which she placed the potatoes. Then, she covered them up with ash and glowing coals.

Adam watched approvingly then he went to untie his sleek black greyhound hunting dog from its tether on the rear of the wagon. As soon as he untied his dog, it bolted off into the depths of the forest. With no time to say goodbye to his wife, Adam glanced back at her. He then spun and trotted off in pursuit of his dog.

Adam was not the only one who has his mind set on a juicy hare for dinner, for unseen by Adam across a clearing in the woods, the property owner Judge Horatio Kingsley and two of his lackey servants had formed a hunting party. Judge Kingsley was called by the Gypsies, "*Naishado Gairo*"(The Hangman), for his habit of sentencing numbers of Gypsies to death for horse stealing whether they were innocent or not.

The judge's face grew flaming red as he forced his way through the low bushes along the edge of the forest clearing. He was followed by his two glum gamekeepers, both deadly serious about the business of being the executioners of the first hares that the judge flushed with his headlong forays into this bush and that. A flash of gray and the judge pointed his finger and bellowed an order to his flunkies, "Fire you imbeciles!" But the flash of gray continued zig-zagging across the field out of their range.

Suddenly to their astonishment, a bolt of black followed closely behind it. "What's that?" the judge blurted as the wiry and graceful Gypsy hunting dog tackled the hare. With one swift bite to its neck, the canine hunter stopped the creature's struggle for life. As the dog carried its kill back to his unseen master, the furious judge shouted, "God, Blimey, it's a wretched Gypsy coursing dog. There must be some vagrants camped here abouts!"

Kingsley hesitated for a moment, clenching his fists and watching as the dog disappeared over a low rise in the distance with his prey.

The dog dropped the hare at Adam's feet. Adam snatched up the hare's carcass and gave his dog a quick reassuring stroke. Then, they both headed back to camp.

Kingsley shrugged off this temporary interruption of his hunting expedition and continued to rampage through the brush. He was intent that there would be wild game upon his table tonight for he expected several important guests. Which included George Whitney, a Southamptom minister and the fiancee of his beautiful daughter Rebecca.

Kingsley grunted as he kicked a hollow log which lay before him. To his amazement, two large hares emerged from the end, they ran right in front of his keeper's shotguns. These much maligned keepers were not about to disappoint their master this time. Two simultaneous blasts from their shotguns find their mark. Kingsley beamed, "Now lads, you're earning your keep."

Adam was startled by the reports in the distance. He and his dog hastened back to camp with the hare in hand.

Kingsley's head keeper reached down and grabbed the largest of the dead hares. He held it by it's ears, lifted it up and proudly displayed it to Kingsley. "You are finally worth your salt, Williams. Now, let's see if you can skin them as well as you can shoot them."

Having been slightly salved by the hunting successes of his servants, the indignant Kingsley was only momentarily humored, for he was the kind of man who could not let the presence of trespassers on his land go unpunished.

When he had made it back to his estate, he gave an order to his lackeys, "Harness my blasted trap and bring it up to the house. We must find out to whom that infernal canine belongs!"

Kingsley pulled his bulk up into the seat of his two wheeled cart and started off down the lane, while his two servants ran behind him.

Adam sensed their presence as they approached the camp. He sent his dog off into the woods with a low whistle and a hand signal, he then tucked the hare beneath a nearby brush pile.

When he reached the camp, the judge hopped out of his wagon and bulldogged his way up to Adam's face. "Do ya know that you are camped on my property?"

"Yes sir, I do know that this is private land but I had to stop. You see my child is very sick with a fever."

Adam pointed to the low bender tent where his wife held the sick child. "I'll be on my way as soon as my child is well. , If you'll accept, I will pay you for the use of this spot."

The judge was little affected by Adam's problem. He grunted and spoke, "Take care of the boy tonight, but I don't want to catch the sun shining on your miserable family tomorrow." He climbed back into his wagon and grabbed hold of his reigns. He stared back with seriousness into Adam's face and repeated his warning, "Heed my word Gypsy, I have no patience for your kind."

The judge's party were now nearly out of sight. Adam called back his dog. They both watched as the judge and his two footmen disappeared into the gloom of the slowly darkening forest.

Adam recovered his hidden hare and brushed the loose dirt from its fur. He drew a knife from his pocket and proceeded to clean it. Having skinned and gutted the hare, Adam washed the carcass in a bucket of spring water. He rewarded his faithful dog by cutting two small joints of meat from the hare's legs. He tossed the morsels to his dog and praised him. "There, boy, now that's a *coushta jook*(good dog)." The dog wagged its tail in appreciation then it devoured the small portions of hare, crunching loudly as it chewed the meat and bone.

Adam placed the rest of the hare on a board and cut it up into smaller pieces. He carried it over to Vashti who put it into a pot of simmering onions, carrots, and her own wild herbs.

As Vashti poured a small stream of spring water from a pail, Adam held his hands beneath it while he washed the blood and gore from his fingers. He dried his hands on his lambskin pants, then he walked a short way and leaned down to look inside his tent where young Tom was resting. "How is my boy doing?" Tom rose and walked into his father's arms. "Why you are soaking wet? Your fever has broken, so let's go see what mother has cooked for us."

Adam and Tom sat cross legged on a blanket as Vashti served them their simple, but delicious, meal.

At Kingsley's estate on the other side of the woods, his guests had arrived, the servants were scurrying about. They had been busy preparing the dinner and setting the fine china service on a massive Jacobean table in his majestic dining hall. A servant girl ladled hare stew into a fine china bowl as Kingsley, his daughter Rebecca and her fiance, the Reverend George Whitney, seated themselves at the table beside two other guests.

Whitney smiled, as he inhaled the delicious steam that arose before him. He commented. "Sir, I dare say if this stew tastes half as good as it smells, I will be forever in your debt for honoring me with this elegant meal."

Rebecca started in, "George, did you know that Father has procured our meal from a forest hunt this very afternoon?"

"Is that so, Sir?"

Judge Kingsley puffed up with pride. "Oh my, it's nothing to brag about, Reverend. It is not a fallow deer, just a couple of old hares, but it seems of late that they are becoming scarcer and harder to come by. Why, I can remember when there was a constant supply of rabbits and hares around before there were so many Gypsies and poachers mucking about."

Whitney replied, "It would seem sir, that the Gypsies were doing the local farmers a favor by keeping the rabbits in check thereby increasing the cabbage and vegetable production."

The judge gruffly countered, "Our sportsmen could handle the job just as well. We have enough indigenous lowlife with which to contend, let alone having to deal with a people who speak gibberish and are made up of the scum of the Earth."

The judge's diatribe irks Whitney. "I beg to differ with you, sir, if you read your histories, then you would know that the Gypsies are a fairly homogeneous people who seldom mix with other races. The language that they speak is akin to Hindi and Sanskrit. There are also a few loanwords mixed in from the countries which they passed through in all of the centuries of their travels."

The judge narrowed his eyes and gave Whitney a analytical stare, "Just what is your interest in these outcasts, Mr. Whitney?"

"I am a fisher of souls, sir, when I began my missions I fished for lost souls in Africa and Asia. But little did I know that right in our dooryard there was a multitude of men, women and children who were eager to hear the word of God and seek salvation. Many of these poor souls go to their reward without ever having heard the gospel of the Lord."

"Well, I wish you luck if it is your inclination to waste your time and assets on a band of heathens, for you will well need it. On the other hand, it does kind of comfort one to think that his hen houses are being raided by good Christians instead of godless savages."

"Father, why do you persist in making light of George's work among the poor? He has more than thirty orphans under his care, and he has trained and placed into service many unfortunate young men and women."

"Well, you'll not have any luck placing their services here. Can you imagine horse thief stable boys and young Gypsy wenches handling the sterling service!"

"I think you made your point, father. Before this discussion gets more unpleasant, I'll ask Mr. Whitney if he will say the blessings for our lovely dinner."

In the early morning mist, Adam rose from his pallet beside his sleeping wife and child. He slipped on his boots and quietly exited his tent. His faithful dog greeted him and followed closely as he walked back into the woods to relieve himself. As Adam urinated behind a large oak tree, he noticed that his dog was becoming agitated. Adam turned toward the direction of his dog's interest. He placed his hand before the dog's muzzle as a signal for him to remain silent. They both listened intently to the faint rumblings of two horsemen who approached in the distance.

Adam and his dog stood frozen in silence as the judge's two clumsy gamekeepers approached his camp. Adam tied his dog to a tree and quietly but firmly commanded him to lie down, "*Besh Jook*," and be silent, "*shoon Jook*."

He watched the judge's men as they dismounted and walked towards his camp. Adam, like a phantom, outflanked the men. Then, he followed closely behind them.

When they reached his tent, the lead man kicked over his kettle and shouted, "We gave you fair warning, Gypsy, now we are gonna have to break up your camp!"

Adam bolted into the camp as the larger of the two men began to shake the end of his tent where his wife and child lay sleeping. He grabbed hold of his thick neck and, with his fist, Adam gave him a crushing blow to the side of his head. This sent him crashing into the now cold ashes of the camp fire.

Adam raised his fists in a championship bare knuckles fighting stance. He moved gracefully and his facial expression was that of a predatory animal. He began to menace and circle the keeper who had not yet felt the power of his pile driving fists. The frightened keeper faced Adam in surrender with raised and open palms, "You - you - you are Gypsy Adam, aren't you? Why I won't fight you. You killed a man in the ring in Surrey last year, didn't you?"

Adam answered, "Well, maybe I am or maybe I ain't, but I can sure as hell beat the ears off of you two."

The keeper on the ground pulled himself up and clumsily ambled in Adam's direction. The other keeper quickly got between he and Adam, grabbing him in a restraining bear hug, "No John, it's Gypsy Adam, the man will kill you! Come, let's leave them be."

Adam picked up the injured man's hat and handed it to him. The now wide-eyed keeper nodded respectfully and, as he and his partner walked to their horses, the more sensible one turned to Adam. "We'll tell the judge that you've left. He's in Southampton for business this morning, but he'll be by this afternoon so you had better be off by then."

Young Tom had been awoken by the commotion and had witnessed the conflict. He ran to his father's arms,

11

"My daddy you showed those moushes(men) who was their better, didn't you?"

"Yes, I did my bitta moush(little man)." Adam put his hand on Tom's forehead, "Now there, you feel as cool as a spring trout. Will you help your Daddy get loaded for the road?"

Adam packed up his family and they were soon on the road again. It was dusk when they reached their destination, Marl Pit Oaks, a favorite camping site in the forest near an old pit where local farmers would come to dig the lime rich marl clay to use as fertilizer for their fields.

# Chapter 2

Old Sylvester Boswell sat cross legged on a burlap bag in a clearing in the woods. He enjoyed the warmth of the clear fall sunshine on his body. From a pile of thick willow rods, he deftly whittled clothes pegs for his wife Richanda to peddle to nearby farm wives.

He had tied white rag bandages on several of his fingers to cover and protect the many small cuts that his razor-sharp pen knife had inflicted upon his quickly moving fingers. This a testimony to the hazards of his rustic trade.

Sylvester was affectionately called by his younger relatives, "Uncle Wester." This included Adam Stanley. Adam was the son of Wester's long dead first cousin Richard Stanley. Uncle Wester was a true Romnichel, an English Gypsy of the old order.

As Uncle Wester inspected a fresh crimson wound on the end of his right thumb, "Well there! My sweet mother! That's enough for *mandy's kucker*(myself) today! I'm getting so *doddle*(feeble) I can't tell the thumb from the peg."

He wiped his wound, artfully tying another rag bandage to his thumb then he started to clean his work area.

He took the neat little piles of white clothes pegs and stacked them uniformly in the bottom of a willow basket.

Uncle Wester arose from his prolonged work position, moaning as he straightened his back and turned his head towards the sound of barking dogs. It was nearing dusk and someone was approaching the camp.

Adam had reached his planned destination. What a relief he thought to himself when he saw several threads of white smoke rising above the treetops ahead, signaling the location of his relatives' camp.

There arose a curious din as they approached the camp, a mixture of dogs barking and the voices of excited female relatives. Little Tom felt better now. He jumped down from the wagon and ran ahead to greet his big brother, seven year old Levi, who was accompanied by the Wharton boys (his cousins).

Uncle Sylvester greeted Adam, "Get down from there, my nephew, come and have some tea with me."

"I will, uncle, but let me take care of my *gry(horse)* and wagon."

"Nephew, Nephew, let the *chavies* do that. Come let's *rokker(talk)*, and you *pooker*(tell) me all the news."

"*Auva*(Yes) uncle, but let me tie the *gry* out and give him a bit of *pani*(water)."

Uncle Wester nodded and as he turned to walk away, "Take care of your business and when you are done, bring Vashti and the *chavies* over to our *tan* (tent), Aunt will have *hobben*(food) for us all."

Adam found a nice level spot to set up his tent. Just as he finished securing the last peg in the felt covering, his son Levi came running up and gave him a big hug. "Daddy, what did you bring me from the downs?"

Adam smiled at Levi, "Didn't I tell you that if you

didn't come with us that little Tom would get all of the treats and gewgaws at the fair?"

"No Daddy." Levi protested, as his big, brown eyes began to fill with tears.

Adam continued,"You didn't listen and you ran away from us because you wanted to stay with your cousins. Now, do you think that you deserve a prize for treating us like that?"

"No, Daddy. I don't want no prize, I'm just happy that you and Mammy and Tommy are back."

Adam reached into his pocket and pulled from it a bright red, wooden spinning top and a nice white knotted string. He handed it to Levi. "Here, my boy, your dad would never forget you. Now let's see if you can spin a factory-made top as good as you can spin the old one that Uncle Wester carved for you."

Levi reached into his pocket and pulled out his old worn homemade top and dirty frayed length of string. He handed it to Tom, who took it with little ceremony and thrust it deeply into his pocket.

Tom watched with rapt attention as his older brother expertly wrapped the gleaming white string in coils around the bright red top. He put a loop on his middle finger, placed the top firmly in his palm, then whipped it out upon the smooth hard-packed clay where it danced and spun like a small crimson tornado.

As the top spun out it's last revolutions and tumbled unceremoniously to the ground. A familiar voice drew the attention of Adam and the boys. "Aw Adam! Vel! Vel akai!(Come! Come here!) The hobben(food) is ready."

Adam and his little band walked over to Aunt Richanda's tent. The boys started to run when they saw her spread of "luscious vittles," as Uncle Wester liked to call her meals.

Before they were seated, everyone had to clean their hands in Aunt Richanda's wash basin. She watched closely as Tom and Levi completed the task. Then she handed the boys a towel to dry their hands. "I'll have no chickla bitta chors(dirty little boys) a beshing(sitting) at my mesala(table). You boys kekker(haven't) been scratching your bulls(butts), have you?" Tom and Levi were too young to understand Aunt Richanda's humor. Levi felt offended to be spoken to in such an insulting manner and he felt a need to defend he and his younger brother's honor.

"No, aunt, me and Tom don't do that, I promise, so help me dear Daudi!(dear God). That's something I seen gauja(non Gypsy) boys be doing, but not our Tom and me, na, ah!"

"Well, then, you boys just sit by Uncle Wester and I'll feed you some coushta hobben."

Aunt Richanda had roasted a nice leg of mutton. She sliced it from the spit with great dexterity and heaped steaming portions on everyone's plates.

Alongside the meat, she ladled a small pile of boiled and diced potatoes. The potatoes were drenched in butter and finely chopped garlic with a sprinkling of coarsely ground pepper. But the real treat was still cooking beneath the heaped ashes of her campfire in a cast iron dutch oven.

Adam sat with crossed legs before Aunt Richanda's dining cloth, enjoying his meal. He glanced from his meal and began to study a large mound of ashes that bulged from the side of the campfire. He smiled at his old aunt and she gave him a knowing wink. Then, he asked, "Rice pudding?"

"Yes, and capital rice pudding, just for you my boy. I knowed how much you love your old aunt's rice pudding.

So I went to the farmer and got some fresh eggs, cream and butter so as I could make it for you."

"Thank you my aunt. I don't think that a mother could be as sweet to me as you are."

She smiled, got up from her spot and went to the fire. She dug the gray ashes and red embers from the top and sides of a large cast iron dutch oven. She took an iron hook and deftly lifted the heavy lid off. She angled her hook again and from inside the large open pot. She snagged the bale handle of a smaller iron pot, pulling it out with great effort. Then, she carried it over to a large flat rock and set it there to cool.

Adam had watched his aunt all the while with great interest. "Can't we have some now, aunt?"

No, you know we have to let it cool a bit, otherwise it'll burn the chavies moeys(children's mouths)." Adam was disappointed, but he knew the rules. His aunt watched him squirm impatiently for several minutes, seeming to enjoy this bit of light torture. She then gave in, fully knowing that the contents of the pot could scald the pallet of the toughest man.

She filled her fancy red china bowls with the steaming sweet and spicy pudding, making sure to pour plenty of thick cream on young Tom and Levi's servings to cool them down so they wouldn't burn their mouths.

Adam spooned a bite of the delicious dessert into his mouth and slowly savored it. Adam smiled at his aunt, "Oh aunt, you even put raisins in it, kauva kuver's cushty(this stuff's good)."

# CHAPTER 3

It sounded like a rifle shot when the dead limb that Adam was pulling on finally snapped loose from the gnarly oak tree that spread out behind the several Gypsy tents. Adam dragged it over near to his campfire and, with several forceful strokes of his ax, he cut it into more manageable pieces to fuel his fire.

After a little while, the campfire was casting a magical glow upon the leafy canopy above the camp. Adam sat beside the fire and he placed his arm around Vashti as Tom and Levi played nearby like forest sprites.

Uncle Wester approached with a greeting. *"Sar shan, sos me chavis kerring ta rati?"* (Hello, how are my children doing tonight?)

"Just fine, uncle, do sit down for a spell."

Uncle Wester pulled his long swag pipe from his pocket and he sat down on a log near the couple. The boys stopped playing and focused their attention on Uncle Wester as he took a pinch of tobacco from his poke. He loaded his pipe and lit it with the end of a flaming stick he had grabbed from the fire.

As puffs of smoke began to issue from Uncle Wester's lips, the boys settled on the ground close to where he sat. They knew that Uncle Wester was the best storyteller in New Forest and they didn't want to miss a thing. Levi reached up and tugged on Uncle Wester's sleeve, "Uncle, will you tell us some stories?"

Uncle Wester took another puff from his pipe and asked, "What kind of story would you like to hear?"

"Uncle, tell me about where did us Gypsies come from?"

"Well, child, you see when God made the world and all the animals, he was kind of lonely like. So, he started a fire in his big oven and he made himself up a great batch of dough. He made three men out of the dough and he put the first one in the oven to bake."

Levi asked, "Was he gonna eat 'em, uncle?"

"No,no,no, he was gonna cook them and bring them to life. Now he took the first man out too soon before he was really done. He was the white man, you know what we calls the '*gauja moush*'. Now the next one, God left him in the oven too long and he got too done. He is the black man, what we calls the '*kaula moush*'. The last man that he cooked came out just right to a light brown. He was the Gypsy, us '*Romnichels*.'"

Little Tommy, who had been chewing on a crust of bread, looked at it with disgust and threw it into the fire.

Adam asks Uncle Wester a question, "Uncle, is it true that our people come from Egypt?"

Uncle Wester answered, "Well, that's what the old people believe, but I met some Hindu merchants in London once and I was bargaining with them. I was trying to buy this big, beautiful knife from them. They was haggling with me and arguing back and forth between themselves and they kept calling the knife a '*churi*' the same as in our language. So, I asked them to count to five." Uncle Wester raised his hand, flicking his fingers one at a time, "*Ek–do–tin-char–ponge*." This revelation had drawn the interest of all present. "So I counts back at em in Romanus, *Yek–dui–drin–star–pange*." Then, I asked them their word for hair - they said '*bal*'. They said face was '*mu*', 'pani' was water and 'kala' was black. Their words was almost identical to ours. Now these fellows got all excited like and grabbed my hand and called me Panjabi. I tells them no, I'm a Gypsy. It was comical, so no I don't think that we come from Egypt. I tried to talk to one of those Egypt fellas who the old Colonel brought back from Egypt as a servant and his talk sounded like pure gibberish to me."

The next day, Adam bided his time as he awaited the arrival of his younger brother Charles. He had last seen Charles at the Epsom race course in the company of John Cobb the butcher and Sam Anniston the gambler and jockey, two people for whom Adam had neither respect or any use. Adam had grabbed his brother Charles at the racecourse and dragged him aside, cautioning him about associating with these men. Still, Charles would not listen and he continued in their bad company.

Adam's worry turned to concern when Charles finally arrived at the camp leading several fine looking horses.

"Where did you get these blooded horses from, Charles?"

"Brother, is this how you greet me after such a long parting?"

"I should greet you with my fist. From where did you get these blasted beasts?"

"I bought them from Sam Anniston and his brother-in-law Squire Finley. In–."

Adam interrupted, "Squire Finley? He has no stock. Everything he had has been sold off, the man is on the verge of going to the workhouse. What did you pay him for this blooded stock?"

"I paid him a hundred pounds."

"You know as well as I, brother, that these fine stallions are each worth hundreds of pounds. Take these horses far away from the camp and release them for God's sake. I will share your losses, brother!"

"A fine Gypsy you are, Adam. I have a receipt, and if you are afraid, I'll tie the horses off away from the camp. I need the money that these grys will bring. I don't have *vongar*(money) like you do. I will need what these horses will profit me for the coming winter, to take care of my wife and our bita chavy. Tomorrow my Charlotte will arrive with her mother and then I'll leave you in peace."

"Go then, my *divia*(crazy) brother who risks our necks for the sake of his stomach. *Gaver*(hide) your *grys* in the wood so the *gaujas* won't find them."

Charles, in a sullen mood, fed and watered the stallions before he led them off into the forest.

He returned at dark and retired to a pallet that Aunt Richanda had prepared for him beneath her and Uncle Wester's wagon.

During the night the horses could be heard neighing in the distance, frightened by the creatures of the forest.

Early the next morning, as the first tinge of tangerine light rose above the horizon, a stout farmer trudged by the camp on his way to town. He was moving along at a good pace until his progress was arrested by the sounds of the distressed horses in the distant wood. He forced his broad body through the heavy brush that at times sprang back at him, stinging his face, until he finally arrived at the site of all of the commotion.

Charles, in his haste, had tied the horses near the den of a ferocious mother badger. As the horses trampled the soil over her brood's den, she rushed from her burrow and defensively attacked the animal's legs.

She was holding the panicked horses at the end of their tethers with her snarling and bared teeth.

The farmer reached down and with great effort, he grabbed a sapling and snapped it from its base. He took the leafy branch and swung it to and fro, driving the feisty badger back into her den.

The farmer tried to calm the agitated horses, "Now settle down, my lovelies, your troubles will soon be over."

Though the badger stayed out of sight, it took several minutes of gentle rubbing and talking to settle the wild-eyed horses back down to where the farmer could release them from their taught ropes.

The farmer led the horses to a nearby farm where he left them in the care of the farmer. He hurried to Southampton where he raised the alarm and returned with the constable and several deputies.

The farmer led the motley party through the woods to where the horses had been tied, "I found them here gentlemen, tied out to a tree over a badger's den. Look there now, the brocken's already dug out her den entrance where the horses had trampled it."

After thoroughly showing and describing the scene of his remarkable discovery, the excited farmer led the constable and his men onward to the lonely farm where the horses were stabled.

The constable and Quimby, one of his deputies, who was also a local auctioneer, examined the horses. "Quimby, you were there when they inventoried Squire Finley's estate for the bankruptcy sale. Are these the stolen horses?"

"Yes, Sir, I'm sure of it.

"We have Finley's nephew Sam Anniston in custody. He tells us that some Gypsies were responsible for the theft."

The farmer listened with great interest. He became excited upon hearing the mention of "Gypsies." He raised his eyebrows and spoke, "Gypsies, you say? Sir, I passed some Gypsies this very morning. They were camped at Marl Pit Oaks."

The constable perked up. "Anniston said that he passed the horses on to a Gypsy named Stanley. Maybe we shall find him there."

The constable and his men gathered up the horses and proceeded to Adam's camp.

The dogs began to bark as the constable's party approached Adam's camp. Adam knew what was coming. He had a sinking feeling in his stomach as he looked into the troubled eyes of his younger brother Charles. Not a word passed between them as they stood and awaited the oncoming wave of hostility.

The constable strode aggressively toward Adam and confronted him. "Would you know as to whose horses these are? And why they were tied at such a lonely place in the forest?"

Adam, in deep thought, stared at the constable for a moment and before he was able to reply, Charles broke in. "They are mine, purchased fair and square. I have a receipt. I tied them away from the camp because we have a mare in heat here and the commotion of the excited stallions was keeping the whole camp awake."

"Well, we'll see about that. Sam Anniston, the jockey,

has taken Squire Finley's blooded horses and passed them off to some accomplices, a butcher and a young Gypsy, going by the name of Charles Stanley!"

Charles bolted at this revelation, he sprang onto the back of Adam's horse and disappeared down the lane. The angry constable and his deputies subdued Adam and shackled his hands.

Vashti, who had been standing nearby, rushed to Adam's side. "My husband had nothing to do with this, his brother just came upon us last night."

The constable smiled mockingly at Vashti, "Well Ma'am, that don't sound much of an alibi for your man. One of my men here says that he saw you telling fortunes at Epsom downs where this all took place."

Charles rode off at a quick pace. He had traveled a good distance and was nearing a narrow bridge. Approaching the bridge from the opposite direction was a wagon carrying two constables and a prisoner. They were on their way to Winchester and their prisoner was none other than Sam Anniston.

Sam was crouching down on his knees behind the constables. He warned the constables when he saw that it was Charles Stanley approaching. "That's gypsy Stanley the horse thief right there. I'm innocent, he's the one you want."

Charles had escaped his accusers earlier so he had little fear that these lawmen coming from the other direction had any knowledge of his situation.

Charles and the constables acted nonchalantly as they approached each other and the bridge from opposite directions. Neither party wanted to alert the other of the strategic secrets that they possessed. Charles nodded his head while passing slowly between the wagon and the wooden rails of the bridge. As he came alongside the wagon and caught a glimpse of Sam Anniston's face, one of the stout constables drew up a long cudgel from the floor of the wagon. Jumping to his feet, he struck Charles with a crushing blow to the back of his head.

When Charles came to, he was lying in the back of the jostling wagon, chained hand and foot to Sam Anniston who was laughing at his misfortune. Charles bent his head down into his lap, raising his chained hands he felt the back of his aching head. Pulling his hand back, he realized that it was painted with blood.

Sam Anniston was amused at Charles' suffering, "Hey Gypsy, that's quite a goose egg you got there on your noggin."

Charles stared in disbelief into the face of Sam Anniston, his so-called friend and sometimes business partner. He knew that Sam was a cheat and a scoundrel, but they had always dealt with each other on a friendly or mutually respectful basis. At this moment, he finally realized the wisdom of his older brother's warnings.

"You dirty, rotten, lying bastard."

Sam continued mocking and laughing at Charles. Charles swung his wrist chains up over Sam's head and wrapped them around his neck. "I'll show you - now laugh at me!" Charles began to choke the life out of Sam. The rattling wagon drowned out the sounds of Sam's gurgling and struggling for his life. Suddenly, Sam rolled a bit and kicked one of the constables in the back. The constable turned around and began to beat Charles with his long cudgel until Charles was again unconscious. The constable turned to his mate, "I should have let the Gypsy kill that bastard, and save the courts some trouble."

The wagon soon overtook Adam's arresting party.

"Got room for a brother lawman and another Gypsy horse thief in that wagon?"

"I think we have, but you'll have to sit in the back with them, because these gentlemen need a little supervising."

Adam was thrown into the back of the wagon beside his battered brother Charles. The newly added constable climbed into the back of the wagon, kicked Sam Anniston over into a corner and accommodated himself as the wagon started down the road followed by the walking deputies.

# CHAPTER 4

From the time that the constable had arrived and left with the hapless Adam, there was much distress and disorder in the camp at Marl Pit Oak. All of the other families had left the site for fear they might be arrested for complicity or have their horses and property confiscated.

Charles' young wife Charlotte and her old mother Mary had arrived shortly after the ordeal and stayed with Vashti and her boys. They are the only inhabitants of the once lively campsite.

The women traveled to Southamptom the following morning, in order to consult with an attorney who was known to the Romany.

"Ladies, I am sorry to have to tell you this, but, from the evidence, and the reports I have heard from those close to the case, I don't see any possibility of your men getting leniency from the court."

The attorney gave them a paper with his fee written boldly across it. "I will do my best if you wish my help, but I will take my fee up front."

The women fished in their pockets and came up with

half the amount. "Sir, we have but five pounds." The gold coins were snatched from Vashti's hand by the greedy attorney within a split second.

"On second thought, madam, I'll take this deposit and expect the balance after the trial."

George Whitney awoke at his mission. He had his tea and breakfast, then he walked to the post office to collect his mail. He was surprised to find a letter from the Sheriff's chaplain, a Mr. Edward Thompson who happened to be an old friend with whom he had gone to divinity school. The letter read:

"Dear Whitney,

I wish to call your attention to a trial forthcoming that involves two Gypsy brothers who have been charged with horse theft. I have talked to these poor fellows and they said that you were acquainted with their people. They asked me to contact you so that you may offer them help. I think that it may be of benefit if you come and speak with them.

Sincerely,
Edward Thompson."

Whitney folded the letter and placed it in his pocket. He walked back to the orphan school to find Rebecca Kingsley teaching sewing lessons to some of her students.

"Rebecca, I have something to discuss with you concerning a court case that your father will preside over at the upcoming quarter sessions."

" Yes, George, but how could this concern me?"

"There are two Gypsy men who have been arrested for stealing horses and they may be capitally convicted. I plan to go to the trial next week and your presence may affect the outcome of the case. In the very least, it may temper your father's judgement and keep these men from being hung."

"I will be glad to do what I can, George, however, I don't think I can have any influence on my father. If his mind is set, then nothing on earth can change it. But I will certainly try to do what I can, and maybe give some comfort to their families."

As the court session opened, the prisoners were brought out. Sam Anniston was brought before the judge to answer the charges against him. "Your Honor, The charges against me are all lies. Why would I sell my uncle's horses to this Gypsy? I had no right or title."

"The document speaks for itself. Is this not your signature affixed to it?"

"Sir, someone copied my signature. I have never seen that paper."

"It's no use, Mr. Anniston, you were seen in the company of the Gypsy Charles Stanley and the Butcher Cobb at the Epsom Downs during the derby. Several witnesses have now testified to it. Mr. Anniston, you are a disgrace to England and your much-respected family. I am sentencing you to transportation of the penal colony of Botany Bay for the term of seven years at hard labor."

Sam Anniston was led away in chains. Adam and his brother Charles are now brought before the Judge. "Gypsy Adam Stanley, what do you say to the charges that you aided and abetted your brother Charles in the theft and attempted disposal of these horses?"

"Sir, I can only say that I am innocent, and I leave my fate to your mercy."

"Mercy! Do you Gypsies have any mercy when you

steal the livestock of honest and hard-working English-men? Or when your fortune-telling women purloin sil-verware from our foolish maidservants while filling their heads with silly notions?"

"Lord, I can no more help being a Gypsy than a dog can help being a dog. All dogs are not bad and vicious, just as all Gypsies are not thieves and swindlers."

"True, but that may not be the case here as the sto-len horses had been found in the communal possession of you Gypsies. And, as a tame horse is by nature a captive horse, are you trying to tell me that they were hiding in the woods near your camp by their own free will?"

There was slight laughter in the gallery and the judge nodded in reply to the appreciation of his callous wit. "Stanley, I will show some mercy on your account, being that you were not directly involved in the theft, you have a wife and two small boys who are innocent. Adam Stanley, you are sentenced to five years of hard labor to be served aboard one of the Hulk prison ships anchored at Ports-mouth. Take him away."

Vashti and her sons had witnessed the judge's callous treatment of Adam from the back of the gallery. Vashti began to cry as the sentence was read, while Tom and Levi tried to comfort her. Young Tommy did not realize what this all meant. "Mammy, are they gonna put me dad inside one of those great black ships in the *bora pani*(great water)?" "Yes, my child, but we may be able to see him again. And after a long time we will have him back with us."

Now Charles stood alone before the judge. His young wife Charlotte, with her babe in arms and her mother, had pushed their way to the front of the crowd. They were hoping to elicit mercy for Charles by their presence. The judge focused on Charles. "Now Charles Stanley, we have the evidence of several eye witnesses, and the document in your name claiming that you made a payment for a token sum of money for very valuable stallions which were clearly not the property of the seller. Therefore, it is plain to see that you are guilty of the theft of these horses by complicity. You were in the process of transporting them for disposal when you were arrested with the property. What do you have to say to the charges?"

"My Lord, can you not see that these men that I dealt with are dishonest and not men of honor. I admit that I bear responsibility for having the bad judgement to deal with them, but I did pay good coin for these horses which I thought were the property of these men."

"Stanley, let the record show that there has been a theft of valuable property, and that valuable property was found in your possession. I sentence you to death by hanging. The sentence is to be carried out in a fortnight."

Charles' young wife Charlotte let out a gasp, "No! You can't! Please Sir, don't!"

The judge seemed perturbed by Charlotte's outburst of grief. "I'll have order in this court. Bailiffs, remove that woman." But another drama unfolded before they could act.

Charles fell to his knees, raising his hands and his eyes to the judge. "Oh, my Lord, spare my life!"

"No, you can have no mercy in this world. I and my brother judges have come to the determination to execute horse thieves, especially Gypsies, because of the increase of this crime in these locals."

Charles continued to beg while still on his knees. "Do my lord, save my life. Do for God's sake, for my wife's sake, for my baby's sake."

"No," replied the Judge. "You should have thought of your wife and child before. You can ask for forgiveness from your heavenly judge. I am done with you. Now take him away."

Charles was grabbed by the bailiffs and drug away while still on his knees.

Charlotte and her mother were traumatized by this tragic display, they collapsed crying into each other's arms. Rebecca and Reverend Whitney were visibly shaken too.

Though Rebecca had placed herself in the front of the gallery, her presence was ignored by her father, who seemed perturbed by her presence. "I cannot believe the heartless statements that my father uttered to that poor man. I can't believe we are of the same blood."

Rebecca and Whitney walked out of the court building to find the two women in tears. "What will we do now, Mother?" said Charles wife.

Old Mary held the baby and spoke softly to the younger woman,"Don't cry, child, you have this dear little baby to take care of now."

Whitney approached the women and spoke, "What can I offer you poor ladies? I can only tell you that God works in mysterious ways. As sad as these circumstances are, I hope that others of your people learn from this tragedy and draw closer to Jesus."

Old Mary took offence at Whitney's remark. "Sir, we do love Jesus, but where is Jesus now when we need him most?"

"You mustn't feel that way about our Savior, for he is here right now to comfort you."

"Tell him to go away. Now!" cried Charlotte.

Whitney stopped his sermonizing. "I'm so sorry for you poor women. If you would come to my mission in

Fareham, I will take care of you and see that of your needs are met and that your child is given nurture."

Old Mary grabbed hold of Reverend Whitney's hand and she looked him directly in the eye. "Sir, we appreciate your kind offer and we will think on it."

As Whitney was saying his farewells to the women, he encountered Vashti and her boys who were just exiting the courtroom. Tears were streaming down her cheeks.

Whitney stopped Vashti and offered her consolation. She looked at Whitney,"What will we do now? My boys need their father. I need their father."

"Now don't cry my dear lady, there is still hope where there is still life. Do you know of the infant's school and mission at Fareham?"

"Yes, Sir, I do. I have passed it many times and I have heard of your good work there for my people."

"Well, would you please come to my service on Sunday and bring your children? There will be several of your people there who are resident with us and we would like to help you in any way that we can."

"Sir, I am sorry that at this moment I cannot think or speak in my usual manner. I am so very troubled at this time. But I promise to do my best to be there, and I thank you for your kind words."

Sunday morning was bright and warm for an early winter day. Whitney greeted the local people who made their way into his small chapel. He was hoping to see if the unfortunate Gypsy women would take him up on his invitation, he was happy when the soon-to-be young widow appeared with her old mother and her baby. But it troubled him that Vashti and her boys hadn't shown up.

Whitney gave a special sermon which he had written with the Gypsies in mind. Hoping it would comfort them and make them feel welcome. The sermon had the desired effect, Charlotte and her mother agreed to stay at the mission and accept Whitney's hospitality.

Monday morning dawned with a bite of frost in the air. Ice crystals covered the weeds and dry grass. Whitney harnessed his horse to his gig and made his way out to Marl Pit Oak to check on Vashti's welfare.

When Whitney arrived at the camp he was surprised to see that a squad of constables were there to impound Adam's horses and wagon by order of judge Kingsley.

He watched in horror as Vashti argued with a beefy bailiff who tried to untie a beautiful white stallion from its tether. "You have no right! This horse is my property!"

The man paid no attention to Vashti. He proceeded to untie the horse but was angry that the rope was still firmly in her grasp. With all of his might, he tried unsuccessfully to jerk the rope from her grip.

Vashti jumped between he and the horse. He pushed her to the ground and yelled as he pounded on her back, "Why you filthy, Gypsy witch! Let go of it."

This commotion startled the horse. It reared up and began to kick out. One of the kicks caught Vashti on the back of her head, knocking her to the ground. She now lay still in a crumpled heap.

The sheriff slapped the bailiff aside. He knelt to assist the unconscious woman and examine her injuries.

"She shouldn't have done that!", shouted the agitated bailiff. "It's the woman's fault, not mine."

The sheriff looked up at his man. "The deed is done, now go for a doctor. I don't want to hear your excuses - go!"

The boys broke free from the grasp of one of the constables who had been restraining them. They ran to where their injured mother lay. They panicked at the sight of her.

Whitney ran to the spot. "Get this woman to her tent."

Vashti was placed on her bed on the floor of the tent. Whitney took a cloth soaked with water, washing the grime and blood from her face. He examined the gash on the back of her skull. He tore some bandages from cloth towels, wrapping and tying her head up to try to stop the bleeding.

The sheriff and his men stood around all the while, curious to see if Vashti would live or die.

Vashti regained consciousness as the cool, wet cloth flowed across her face. "My boys - where are my boys?" She focused her eyes to see that they were standing beside Whitney.

Whitney knelt beside her and took her hand in his. "Your boys are just fine, my dear. We have sent for a doctor and we are all here to help you now."

"Please, sir. Don't let them take my boys to the workhouse."

"Don't worry, I am here to help you and your boys. If they have to go anywhere, they will go with me to the infants' school where they will be well taken care of. Now my dear woman your wounds are serious. Will you pray with me for your salvation so that you may receive Jesus' mercy?"

" Yes, Sir, but let me see my boys now."

The boys nestled by their mother and tried to comfort her. "My babies, you know that your mother loves you very much." Vashti looked up at Whitney. "Sir, I will say your prayer with you now if you promise me that you will take care of my boys and raise them to be good men like yourself."

"I will."

"And will you give me your word that you will take them to visit their father, when you can, for he dearly loves them?"

"Yes, I will. I will do all in my power to see that they learn to be good and decent men. They will be taught a vocation so that they can earn a living."

Whitney's words seemed to comfort Vashti. A smile came across her face, her eyes slowly closed and as he uttered the Lord's prayer, life passed from her body.

Vashti's boys began to cry as Whitney placed a cover over Vashti's lifeless face. He gathered them in his arms and led them from the tent.

The sheriff and his constables had been standing by the tent's opening and all had witnessed Vashti's passing.

Whitney stopped before the men and addressed them, "Brave men! You can go home now to your wives and children." Whitney stood for a moment, staring them down while gauging their reactions to see if any Christian charity or remorse was left in these callous enforcers of what he saw as an unjust system of law.

The men stood silent, some with their heads down in shame as Whitney continued his diatribe, "Can any of you tell me who be neighbors unto these?"

The sheriff and his men then went about their business of confiscating Vashti's possessions and her lifeless body.

# CHAPTER 5

Whitney helped the weeping boys into his buggy and they began the sad journey back to the mission. When he returned he was greeted by Rebecca and some of the mission residents. "They killed their mother, what a cruel and heartless cabal."

"Who killed their mother?"

"It was an accident. The sheriff was there to impound her horse and possessions to pay fines. The poor woman was kicked in the head by a horse. There was a scuffle with a bailiff while she was trying to protect her property. But this never would have happened if your father was not such a heartless administrator of justice."

"Bring the boys into the kitchen and we'll discuss my father later. These little fellows need our attention now more than anything."

Rebecca brought the boys into the big, warm kitchen and sat them on a bench before the fireplace. She took warm water from a kettle and poured it into a wash basin, washing their faces and hands.

"Are you boys hungry?" Levi answered, "Mother gave

us vittles, but that was a long time ago, ma'am."

"Well I'll see what Aunt Betty has left over in her pantry."

Rebecca brewed the boys some tea which she sweetened and added cream too. As the boys sipped the warming liquid, she sliced scones and slathered them with fig preserves. The boys grabbed the scones from her platter and ate them so quickly that Rebecca was thoroughly surprised. "How did you like Aunt Betty's scones, boys?"

"They was wunnerful, miss." Levi answered.

Tom added, "Could we have another, please?"

Levi gave Tom a stern look. "That's not mannerable, Tommy. You should tell the nice lady that you are sorry for being so greedy."

Tommy looked down in embarrassment. If his big brother said it he thought that it must be true.

"I'z sorry mam for being greedy."

"Oh you aren't greedy, Tom, you are just a hungry boy and you can't be blamed for wanting another of Aunt Betty's scones. They are delicious, aren't they? How about some strawberry preserves on the next one?"

The boys were so engrossed in their strange new environment and the delicious treats that for a slight moment, they almost forgot about the tragic events of the day.

Rebecca took the boys upstairs in the rectory and removed their clothing, dressing them in clean night clothes. She tucked them in bed and kissed their foreheads. "Now, you boys go to sleep and don't have any fears. I will be in the next room if you need me."

Tom spoke, "Miss, I'm afraid, I ain't never slept in a house before."

"Don't worry, child, for you'll be safe. Of what are you afraid?"

" Oh, I'm afraid that the walls might fall in on Levi and me. You see, we ain't used to sleeping so close to such high walls."

"Tommy, I can assure you that the walls of this old house have been standing for a hundred years. They are sure to be standing another hundred."

"You sure, Miss?"

"As sure as that big bowl of sweet porridge that Aunt Betty will feed you boys in the morning. Now you go to sleep."

The next morning the boys arose to their strange new surroundings and they enjoyed their promised breakfast. Rebecca helped them get dressed in new school uniforms and shoes. Tommy didn't like his new shoes. "Why do I have to wear these things? They are heavy and hurt my feet and I can't jump or climb trees with them?"

Levi grabbed Tom's arm, "Just wear them, Tommy, you will get used to them. Besides, Dad will think that you are a gentleman when you see him."

"He will? Then I will wear them, just for me Dad."

Rebecca took the boys around the mission and vocational school. She introduced them to the people who worked there and to some of the other children who were residents. Levi noticed some Romany children that he knew. "Miss, do you know that some of the children here are Gypsies too?"

"Certainly, I do. Gypsy children deserve to have an education just like everybody else. They have a right to learn to read and write just like all children."

"I want to write and read and do ciphering, but if a Gypsy gets too much book learnin' then he gets gaujafied, That's what Aunt Richanda says."

"And what does gaujafied mean Levi?"

"Well I don't want to say anything bad or hurtful about your people miss, but it means that you start acting like a gauja."

"Tell me, Levi - is that a bad thing?"

"Not like you, Miss, but other gaujas do dirty things - like washing dirty clothes in their kitchen basins, and letting dogs and cats lick their dishes clean. If a cat or dog ate from Aunt Richanda or my dear mother's dishes, then they would grab the dirty dishes and dash them to bits so as no other Romnichel would eat from them and be mockered by them."

"And What is mockered?"

"That's when a person is so dirty that no other Gypsies wants to eat with them or be around them. They is what you call mockerdy. Being dirty with dirt don't make you mockerdy, but doing dirty things does. Like a woman washing herself or her hair around cooking things, or a woman dragging the bottom of her dress over a man or his food when he is sitting on the ground. I heard from me dad that when Uncle Wester's dear old mother fell with her arse on Uncle Wester's valuable silver tea set, he took his hammer and pounded it into a lump of scrap metal. So you see that being gaujified or mockerdy is a bad thing for us gypsies."

"Yes, Levi, I can see that. We must be very careful not to let you and Tommy become gaujafied."

Levi lets out a sigh of relief. It was not an easy thing for him to share these secrets with an outsider, even a kind loving one.

"Yes, Miss Rebecca, we sure will have to be careful."

Whitney saw to it that Vashti had a proper Christian burial. He brought Rebecca, the children and some of the mission personnel. He had prepared a special sermon and made sure that the boys joined them in prayer for their departed mother.

# CHAPTER 6

Charles Stanley was scheduled to be executed within a week, but there was nothing Whitney could do to help him. Rebecca had tried to intercede on his behalf, but her pleadings fell on deaf ears. It so angered her father that he ordered her, "Leave this house and do not return until you have respect for my judgment and you can honor my integrity."

After some petitioning, Whitney was allowed to bring the boys for a brief visit to the jail before Adam was taken off to the hulks to serve his sentence.

Adam appeared like a defeated and downtrodden man when the cell door opened, but when he saw his boys all dressed up and in the company of the minister, he forced a smile. "My *moushes*, your dad is so happy to see you. What gentlemen you have become."

The boys hugged their father. Tom spoke, "*daddus*, Oh *daddus*, we miss you so much! When will you come and *lel*(get) us?"

"My boys, I would come and get you tomorrow if I could, however, I will have to go somewhere and do a lot of work before they let me be with you again."

"Will it be a long time, dad?"

"Levi, my son, It will be a while, but now I'm not as troubled. I know that you boys will be in the good care of these dear church people."

Adam grabbed Whitney's hand and looked into his eyes. "Mr. Whitney, I have heard what you did for my dear wife in her last moments, and I can see what you have done for my boys. I can never be able to repay you, but I will do my best when I'm able.

Whitney promised Adam that he would bring his sons to see him again no matter where they took him. Whitney had to carry little Tom from the cell crying since he didn't want to leave his father. After his boys had left, thoughts of the loss of his wife Vashti and the eminent execution of his brother Charles sent Adam into deep depression from which he could find no escape.

A week has passed. At noon, Adam and several other prisoners were put into a large van to be transported to the hulks.

The hulks were Royal Navy and old merchant ships which had been decommissioned, stripped of their masts and retrofitted to serve as temporary prisons for the over-flow of convicts in the English prison system.

In 1775, The American Revolution ended Great Brit-ain's practice of using the American Colonies as a dump-ing ground for their criminal offenders. A crisis arose when alternate housing needed to be supplied for thousands of prisoners now crowding the prison system. Many of these criminals were driven by hunger and desperation to com-mit offenses which now would be considered minor, things such as stealing food or articles of clothing.

To solve this problem, a decision was made to retain

in English ports, ships that had been used in convict transportation and to employ them as floating prisons. This was done as a temporary measure but the practice endured for eighty years.

Adam's designated prison hulk was the Victoria which was permanently anchored off the swampy bank of Southampton Water. It was manned by a squad of soldiers and administered by a dozen or so guards and quartermasters.

Adam was stripped of his clothing upon his arrival at the landing grounds. He and his fellow prisoners were roughly shorn of all their hair. They were then placed in wooden troughs of cold water where they were lathered with crude soap and roughly scrubbed all over with coarse bristled brushes.

The prisoners doing the scrubbing found great pleasure in degrading and roughly treating their newly arrived brethren. They laughed incessantly as they mocked and taunted Adam and his companions.

Adam stood silent and shivering as his toothless assailant brutally forced a rough brush across his neck, drawing blood in the process. "Hey mates, look at this one. I've washed him thoroughly and he's still a bit tawny. I think he's gonna need a lot more scrubbing."

His mate answered, "No, I think you're wrong, Weasel. That's about as clean as you are going to get that one, he's a filthy Gypsy. I'd say you did a fair job on him."

Adam had made his mind up earlier that he was going to be as passive as possible while trying to be a good prisoner in order to get his sentence reduced. But these indignities had pushed him past his tolerance level. He grabbed a handful of lye soap in one hand and a fist full of his tormentor's hair in the other, drawing the two together until he was able to grind the caustic soap into the eyes of his tormentor. Weasel screamed like a distressed damsel and dove off of the bank into the cold water where he tried to rinse the burning soap from his eyes.

The prison guards and their helpers laughed heartily at the Weasel's misfortune. Then, a tall muscular guard who seemed to be running the whole show walked over to Adam. "This is exactly the kind of behaviour that we are put here to abolish." He motioned for the guards to hold Adam's arms. He pulled a short leather whip from his pocket and beat Adam about his face, chest and neck until he was covered with welts and blood. "Now take this truant Gypsy and dress him in the coarsest jacket and breeches that you can find. And don't spare the iron when you choose his leg chains."

Adam was led over to a pile of coarse, gray woolen clothing and along with the rest of the new inmates he was outfitted. Then they were taken to a blacksmith who placed permanent shackles on their ankles. Adam noticed that the long chain connecting his shackles was heavier and thicker than those of the other prisoners. A leather belt was given them to hold up their trousers, and a leather strap was added to hold the chain up between their legs from their belt so that the chain did not drag when they walked.

Adam was then taken aboard the hulk where he was given a number by an administrator. "Convict number Five-One

Three, remember this number for you have no name now. You and the other men will be taken below to the lowest part of the hulk where you will be given a hammock and instructions by Mr. Blevins."

Adam and the men passed over the main deck to a narrow stair case that snaked its way down into the bowels of the ship. It took a while for the men's eyes to adjust to the dim light of the lower deck. Each man was given a wrapped bundle which contained his blanket and hammock. These items had been boldly marked with each man's prison number.

They were rudely awakened before dawn the next morning. Then they were taken to the top deck to wash up for breakfast. Their breakfast consisted of porridge and a hunk of pork fat. They were then taken back down to the lower deck where they were instructed to roll up their hammock and blanket and bring them to the storage area.

Adam was then led with his group of prisoners to the top deck and then down the stairs to a landing craft which they boarded. They rowed the craft to the mouth of a small stream which flowed from a great swampy tidal estuary.

"Out of the boat, you bloody bastards!" yelled a tall jailer. He ordered the men to lift two tightly wrapped bundles out of the boat. They struggled to carry the unwieldy bundles over the sides of the boat and as the men found footing on the mucky bank, their feet sunk into the mire below them.

They carried the bundles to a small piece of land which was a bit drier and covered with weeds. A large three-foot deep hole was dug and the coarse material was pulled from the objects to be buried: two naked prisoners, one but a lad of eighteen and the other a muscular brute with the swollen face of a bulldog. Adam was repulsed as were the other prisoners. A bespectacled prisoner, as he helped the others drag the young man to his grave asked the guards, "How did these men die?" The tall guard placed his hand on the back of the questioner's neck and began to squeeze, "The same way that you will if you get romantic with a fellow prisoner or continue to ask questions. Now bury this filth and get back in the boat."

The men were then taken to a site along the solent where they were given shovels and ordered to dig a drainage canal, a project which would last them the rest of the winter.

# CHAPTER 7

Levi was adjusting well to his new life at the mission, but Tom was having problems. Levi had become Rebecca's little helper but Tom felt as if he had been abandoned by his older brother. "She's not our mammy, Levi, she is an ol *gauja*. Why you want to be with her an not me?"

"Tommy, she loves us, she does so much for us."

"She's a filthy *gauja*, and I stole her scissors. I hid them from her. She is not like mammy."

Levi brought Tom to Rebecca the next day. Tom was tearful and sullen, he carried Rebecca's lost scissors in his hand. As he stood quietly before Rebecca, Levi spoke. "Miss Rebecca, our Tom was bad. He stole your scissors."

"Is this true Tom?"

"Yes Miss, I sorry." He handed the dirty scissors to Rebecca. She slowly took them from him and wiped the dirt from them.

"And our Tom did a real bad thing ma'am." Tears flowed from Tom's eyes as Levi continued, "Tom killed a tiny bird in the garden. He threw a rock and hit it. I told him that it was a wicked thing that he done, and that he never should do that to God's little creatures. I made him bury it and say a prayer over it, and for him to ask forgiveness from the little bird's mother and father. They was in a tree over where Tom buried it and they was chirping at him. And then Tom yelled up at them that he was sorry, he cried really hard."

"Well, Tom, it was a terrible thing to kill that poor little bird and to steal my scissors, but if you promise to be good then I will forgive you. And the birds may well forgive you too if you truly are sorry."

"I be real sorry ma'am. I promise."

As the boy's become comfortable with their new lives, Rebecca took it upon herself to teach the boys gentility and proper speech.

Levi was a good student, but she couldn't get the wildness out of Tom. He was forever climbing trees in search of bird eggs, while he roamed the woods and fields finding edible plants and mushrooms which he brought back to the mission. Rebecca did not appreciate Tom's reluctance to civilize, but old Betty the cook gladly took in this natural bounty which she incorporated it into the mission meals.

The arrival of spring was announced by the fragrant blossoms of the Fareham mission fruit trees. Whitney took the boys out into the orchard to give them some good news. "Tom and Levi, you have been good students. I know that it has been hard on you adjusting to a new way of life. Rebecca and I are going to take you to visit your father tomorrow bright and early."

"Oh, Sir, can we bring him gifts of food?"

"Yes Tom, but only small things that he can enjoy while we are there visiting with him. But don't worry, Miss Rebecca has made a nice plum pudding full of nuts and sweetmeats and I have a bottle of ale to help him wash it down."

The boys laughed and ran back to their quarters to prepare their clothing to make sure that they made the best impression possible on their beloved father.

Everyone in the mission gathered to see the prison visiting party off. An old Gypsy woman raised her voice over that of the staff and children, "Tell your daddus Adam that his old aunt wishes him good health and *koushta bok*!(gook luck!)"

Whitney borrowed a team of horses and a fine carriage for the trip to Portsmouth. As he tooled the team along the lane, the little group looked like a well to do family on their way to church.

For the family visit, only the prisoners with very good behaviour were allowed to participate. As a result, only thirty or so of Adam's fellow prisoners qualified for the privilege. The visitation took place in a small park area on the shore in site of the hulk.

When Tom and Levi first spotted their father, they were so excited that they dragged Whitney and Rebecca right through the guards and prisoners until they reached Adam. "Dad, my dadus." Levi wrapped his arms around his father's neck. Tom squeezed his way into the embrace. They all three hugged and cried.

"Daddy, we miss you so much. When are these mushes gonna let you vel home to us?"

"Maybe soon, you boys just keep being good and listen to this dear man and lady. We'll all be back together when the our good Lord wills it."

Levi grabbed his father's hand, "Dad, I got some real good news for you."

"What is it, son?"

"Our Tom can count to a hundred in *gauja*."

"Can you now, Tom?"

"Ya, but I don't want to. And you know Miss Rebecca has teached us to read books. She has told us all of the stories in the Bible, and she wants us to be like *tatchi(true)* gentlemen."

"Well I can see that she is doing a good job of it. You two are truly real gents."

Tom smiled proudly at his father's praise.

"I doubt that you young gentlemen will want to be seen with your ignorant old father when I get out of here."

"You ain't ignorant daddy, no *tatchi Romnichel* is ignorant, only some *gaujas* is."

"My child, some Romnichels are ignorant, just like some *gaujas* are ignorant. You boys remember and don't judge people like they judge us."

Tommy was in deep thought as he analyzed his father's ragged appearance. He pointed to his father's worn and calloused hands. "But Dad, if you were at the mission, Aunt Betty would be sure to pull your ear for having such dirty nails."

"Tommy, I would love for Aunt Betty to pull my ears if she fed me as good as she's been feeding you boys."

Adam felt ashamed of his worn hands and dirty nails. He folded his hands and placed them on his lap so that Rebecca and Whitney couldn't see them.

Rebecca saw that Adam was embarrassed, so she put her hand on his and gave him a warm smile. "Tommy, your father's hands are the hands of an honest, hard-working man. You should be proud of him. He is doing his best to work very hard so that he can be back with you boys sooner."

Adam greatly appreciated Rebecca's kind words and

it lifted his spirits. Rebecca handed Adam the small pudding cake and bottle of ale. Adam was surprised. "Thank you, Miss, it's been some time since I have been treated this well. I want to thank you from the bottom of my heart for what you and Mr. Whitney have done for me and my family. I will be forever grateful to you."

"Mr. Stanley, your boys have been a pleasure to me. They help a lot at the mission."

"Have they been obedient?"

"Yes they have, especially Levi. He loves to learn, and he is a good mechanic. And Tom, Tom is my helper. He helps me with the other children, and he is a great gardener, he loves to see things grow."

They all said their goodbyes and as Whitney's coach disappeared down the lane, Adam wolfed down most of his pudding. He drank what was left of his ale before any of the guards or prisoners had a chance to wrestle it from him.

Adam was about to pop the last piece of the pudding cake into his mouth when he felt a powerful hand on his shoulder. It was his new friend and fellow prisoner, Jacques Rouseau. "Mon Ami, what have you there?"

"Oh Jacques, here my friend. I've had enough, you enjoy." Jacques grabbed the small piece of delicacy and rolled it around in his mouth while savouring the flavor. "Magnifique, mon frere, and what of the beautiful lady who gave it to you? She cannot be the woman of a man like you."

"What do you mean by that? Jacques, I thought that you were my friend."

"I mean, Mr. Five-One-Three. I cannot see you, a Gypsy who steals all zee poultry, from all zee people all zee the time being the lover of such a fine woman."

"Maybe your French Gypsies steal chickens, but if a Gypsy is desperate enough to be a thief here in England, he wouldn't risk his neck for a chicken. Over here we steal the whole chicken farm and the farmer's horse and his wife and his beautiful daughters."

"You Romany-chels. Now I see why they say that you are such great storytellers. I have just been told the greatest fairytale I have ever heard."

"You laugh, Frenchy, but just wait and see. That beautiful lady will one day be mine and the mother of my boys."

"There is nothing wrong with dreaming, Mr. Five-One-Three. I, mon frere, will be the first to congratulate you if this fairy tale comes true."

The powerfully built Frenchman Jacques Rouseau was a leftover from the Napoleonic Wars. He had been captured in a naval battle and, while being imprisoned in the hulks, he fell in love with a local married English woman who visited the hulks with a charity group. When Jacques was released at the end of the war, he remained in England to carry on his clandestine romance with the woman for many years. One day the woman's husband followed her to Jacques cottage in the forest and he caught them together. He attacked Jacques with a club and severely beat him about the head. Barely conscious, Jacques put the man in a bear hug and broke the man's spine, crippling him. Jacques was convicted of attempted murder and the adulterous activity added to the sentence. So, Jacques had by now spent most of his adult life in the British prison system.

Adam's reputation as a pugilist was well-known in the area. When he was admitted to the hulks, word spread rapidly among the guards and prisoners.

Several times a year, wardens and officers from the other hulks and prisons would clandestinely gather to pit the toughest man in their prison against the others. Thousands of pounds were wagered and the men in charge coveted the honor of as they said, "Owning the champion."

At first, Adam was made fun of and taunted by his guards, when the time was nearing for the spring contests, however, Adam's warden (a Mister Hoskins), began to eye Adam up and see to it that his food rations increased in quantity and quality.

This extra attention became the talk of the hulk. One day Adam was sent for and taken by a group of guards to a nearby barn. There he was met by Hoskins and a large, rough-looking prisoner by the name of Ollie Jones. Adam had seen Ollie fight when he was a young man. He knew that he had a reputation as a dirty fighter, and he had been to a fight where Ollie had gouged out the eye of a man who, up until that point, had been getting the better of him.

Ollie was in his late forties and hardly comparable to the image that Adam had of him when he was in his prime. His hair was gone. His eyebrows and the ridge of his nose was naught but scars, and his ears were but misshapen objects hanging off the sides of his head. Still, the fierceness of his stare was still there as well as his powerful trunk and bulging forearms.

Hoskins had the men's wrist shackles removed. "I suppose you know why you are here, Mister Five-One-Three."

Adam looked at Hoskins, "What's in this for me?"

"To start with, let's first see what you have left in you."

The men squared off in the center of the barn. They moved surprisingly well despite the heavy chains and shackles about their feet. Adam landed a glancing blow to Ollie's jaw but it didn't phase him. Ollie pursued Adam around the arena. He lunged towards him and Adam side stepped. Ollie fell and as he did so he grabbed Adam's ankle chains and pulled until Adam was on his knees. Ollie rose up and began to rain violent blows down upon Adam's face.

Adam punched Ollie between his legs and this disabling blow gave Adam time to get to his feet. Both men knew that they were in a life-and-death struggle and prize ring rules scarcely applied here.

Adam started in on Ollie with a combination of jabs and punches. He targeted his jaw, his chin and the sides of his head. Ollie absorbed the full impact of Adam's solid punches and he fell to the floor like a pole-axed steer.

"Bravo, Five-One-Three. I see that you still have it."

This cheered Adam. He felt like a man again. He was getting the respect that he knew he deserved from the top man in this crazy world into which he had been thrown.

"Now, sir, may I ask what you will do for me if I do this for you?" Adam pointed to Ollie who was still unconscious on the ground.

"I'll see to it that you will only have a chain on one ankle and that you work aboard the hulk for a half week and not have to serve on the dredging gangs anymore."

"Thank you, Sir. That is a good start, but I would rather continue to work hard for you and get a shorter sentence if possible. I will fight hard for you and do your bidding."

Hoskins shook Adam's hand. "Here's to our partnership. Let us hope it will be beneficial for the both of us."

# CHAPTER 8

Since her last visit with Adam, Rebecca had been thinking more about her life and her relationship with Whitney. She noticed the way that Adam openly showed his love for his sons and she enjoyed the way that he looked at her. She loved his smile. There was something about his manly smile that Rebecca couldn't get out of her mind. When she went to bed at night her last thoughts were of that smile, and she woke up to thoughts of Adam's smiling face.

Lately Whitney was almost always serious and impersonal with her. Rebecca tried to remember the last time that Whitney had given her a warm and caring smile, or an affectionate embrace. It was hard for her to recollect.

Rebecca had always admired Whitney for his kindness and gentle ways. She also admired the way that he spoke to and treated people no matter their class or station.

They had been engaged for several years now and Whitney always skirted the question whenever she pushed the issue about setting a date for marriage. He brought up his future plans to improve the well-being of one or another of the indigent sectors of people living in the area. Whether it be orphans, children of the local prostitutes or Gypsies in distant parishes.

One day, Rebecca finally confronted Whitney as they rode home from an errand of charity in nearby Southampton.

"You know George, we are not getting any younger."

"Yes, I know that, but isn't a blessing to be allowed the gift of yet another day of life?"

"Yes, of course it is. What I'm getting at is that I am becoming a spinster right before your very eyes."

"Rebecca, what do you mean by that?"

"George, I scarcely can recall the last time you held my hand or kissed me."

"I care for you, Rebecca, but I can't put our comfort and happiness above the poor and suffering who need my attention. One day when the fruits of our labors are ready to be harvested and we have people in place who can take this load off of our shoulders, we will have time to consummate our marriage."

"George, I can see now that you are not the man with whom I fell in love. You put other things and other people's happiness above ours. George, I am a normal woman. I have needs and wants. I would like to have a family one day, and I don't think that you share my feelings."

"Oh Rebecca, please bear with me. I made a vow to myself and the Lord that I would make a success of my mission and school and see that it was self-sustaining before I settled down to have a life and family for myself."

Rebecca slowly removed her glove and slid a thin gold engagement band off of her finger. She looked at it for several seconds and tears welled up in her eyes. Whitney stopped. "Rebecca, what are you doing?"

Rebecca handed the ring to Whitney. "Here, take this and sell it. Use the money for your mission."

"No, Rebecca, don't. I made that ring for you. You saw how hard I worked to beat that gold sovereign into a band while working to shape and polish it. My hands bled from that labor of love."

"Yes, but I don't feel that love now so take it. It means nothing to me."

Whitney took the ring and he placed it in his coat pocket. Rebecca could see that he was hurt, but he didn't say a word to her and remained silent on the trip back to Fareham.

Rebecca put her mind into her work over the next several months. She focused on her role as a teacher for Adam's boys. As the time neared for the next scheduled visit to the prison, Rebecca seemed to have a positive change in her mood, which Whitney sensed every time the subject of the visit was brought up.

Rebecca and Aunt Betty, on the eve of the visit, were having an enjoyable time in the kitchen preparing dinner and a dessert for Adam.

Whitney seated himself at the dining room table beside Tom and Levi, waiting for his food to be served. They all enjoyed a nice bowl of beef stew, cheese and bread. When the meal was finished, Whitney waited in anticipation of the delicious dessert which he had been smelling all while he has been dining.

"Well, I'll have some cream on mine." said Whitney as he sat with his hands folded. Rebecca looked at Whitney and didn't say a word. Little Tom looked up at Whitney and said, "Miss Rebecca said that we can't have no pie. There was only a few apples left in the cellar and she only made a small one. And it will only be enough for me poor dad when we goes to see him tomorrow, so you and me don't get none."

Whitney was hurt, but he wouldn't let Rebecca see it. He now realised that his wants and needs were not as important to Rebecca as they had been. She now thought more of pleasing another man, but was it charity or was she truly interested in this Gypsy - Adam?

Many thoughts were going through Whitney's mind as he helped Rebecca up into the carriage. When he smelled the sweet aroma of lavender and noticed how stylishly she was dressed, he thought she seemed as twittery as a young girl in love for the first time. He had to comment, "Rebecca, you smell very pleasant."

"Oh, that is lavender oil. It was given to me by one of the poor prostitute women we helped at the mission. Dear thing, she scarcely had clothing on her back, but she gave me her most prized possession."

Whitney looked Rebecca up and down. "Don't you think that you are dressed a bit frivolous and flashy to be visiting a prison? You know we must set a good example for others to follow. I think that those are not proper garments for a woman in your position to be wearing. You may give those poor souls at the hulks sinful ideas."

"Were I your wife, other men's thoughts of me might be sinful and covetous. By your choice, George, I am a spinster, and therefore free to occupy the thoughts of any man."

Whitney's lips puckered up as if he had just chewed and swallowed a whole lemon. "I don't know what's gotten into you, Rebecca. But these are not the words nor thoughts of a chaste Christian woman."

"An idle heart yearns for attention. George, even a

puppy will wander afield when its master refrains from petting it."

Levi and Tom felt that something was wrong. They saw that Rebecca was upset so they reached up and placed their small hands on her arm. She looked back at them and smiled.

Whitney observed this and spoke calmly,"I think these matters are better discussed in private. I see no reason to worry the minds of these children with our problems."

"I think so too, George. We can talk more on this matter tomorrow. We will put our differences aside and make this visit pleasant, as it should be."

The prison visit went well, but it was very difficult for Whitney, though he tried not to show it. Adam greeted them warmly, and showered his boys with love. "I want to thank you, sir, for these kind blessings you have brought to me. These visits make my life easier, giving me hope that I will be able to have a future."

Whitney felt shame for his jealous statements to Rebecca about Adam."Mr. Stanley, it is the least that we can do after our people have done you and yours such harm."

"Sir, I don't consider you and Miss Kingsley any part of those people. To me, you have hearts of gold and I can only ever think on you with love and admiration."

With Adam's simple words, Whitney lost any anger, resentment or jealousy that he had for him.

"My dear fellow, I am glad to help a poor soul like you. I take great pleasure in fostering Levi and Tom. They have been good students and you did a very good job as a father teaching them right from wrong. They have been a very good influence on the other children at the mission."

"That is good to hear, for it makes a father proud coming from such a good man as you, Mr. Whitney."

Rebecca and Whitney left the prison on a happy note and, upon reaching the mission, the boys were surprised to see that Uncle Wester and Aunt Richanda had set up camp on the mission grounds.

Levi jumped from the wagon as it slowed to a stop. "Mr. Whitney, why didn't you tell us that Uncle Wester was coming?"

"I wanted it to be a surprise for you boys."

Tom also jumped out of the carriage and the boys ran over to Uncle Wester.

"Uncle! Uncle! We are so glad to see you." They hugged Uncle Wester and he seemed surprised to see them dressed up in their Sunday best.

"What fine gentlemen yous boys have become. Why, if I seen you on the street, I wouldn't even recognize yous. Tell me, Levi, how is your dear dadus *kerring*(doing)?"

"He's doing just fine, uncle. You know he's gonna be down, especially about Mother. He tells me that he thinks about her every day and it's hard on him cause he don't want the other men to see him cry. But he said that the Hulk ain't half so bad as he thought it would be."

"Well, it were awful the things that happened, and me and your aunt didn't hear about it till we were way in Wales up in the mountains. One of the Wharton men heard from a travelling showman who read a newspaper piece to him. So, I came as quick as I heard."

"We miss our dear mother and father, uncle, but there was naught you could have done. It was good that you was gone away. I know aunt would have fought the muscars*(police)*, they would have hurt her or took her up."

"Probably so, my boy, but it was sure a blessing that you boys had the good minister and young lady here to help you. It was ever so nice that the good minister let me and your old aunt camp here so that we could visit and see how you boys are doing."

"Yeah uncle, maybe you can show these *gaujas* how to make clothes pegs and baskets."

"*Shoon, shoon. Kekker pen duver chavy. (Quiet, quiet. Don't say that, child).* If we teach the *gaujas* to make Gypsy things, then what my boy, will we be able to sell them to earn our bread?"

"You are right uncle. Lor I must be thinking like a *gauja*, forgive me. But you and aunt won't have to worry about the *hobben(food)* much. Me and Levi have turned farmers and have a garden patch of lovely vegetables for you to pick when they are ready."

"You hear that, Shander? Your nephews have become Johnny raws."

"We ain't Johnny raws, uncle. We are gentlemen

farmers. Levi told me that Johnny Raws was dumb farm boys with coarse ways."

"I didn't mean anything bad by it my Tom, just making a bit of a joke."

Tom nodded, but his little face still registered a trace of disappointment from what he still perceived as an insult from his beloved uncle.

Uncle Wester smiled and led the boys around in an effort to change the subject. "Yes, this is sure a nice place and it's getting so hard to find a little spot beside the lane to *hatch a tan(pitch a tent)*. With that new Rural Police Force driving us up and down the roads night and day."

Levi showed his maturity in answering Uncle Wester like a man. "Yes, there has been a lot of that lately. They are real *juckals(dogs)* about it too."

"Oh uncle, that reminds me - when the *gavers(officials)* came and *moored(killed)* our dear mother, they took dad's *coushti(good)* coursing *juckal(dog)*."

"Well, Levi, you needn't worry about that jook. Old one-legged Piramus Wells has him filling his stew pot with game. And a good thing it is too, because the poor *moush(man)* has a dozen *chavys*."

"Uncle how ever did Piramus get hold of our *jook*?"

"Seems the *muscar* who *choored(stole)* him from yous had him out on a hunt and was a trying to get him to chase after rabbits, but the *fool* was giving him commands in English."

"Ha - good for him, uncle. That dog don't trust nobody who don't talk like a Romnichel, and he won't do anything for you unless you speak *Romanus* to him."

"Well, let me tell you the rest of the story." Levi nodded and Uncle Wester continued. "When old Piramus *dicked(saw)* the jook, he recognized him and he slunk away. He *lelled* upon his *gry*. He gave a whistle and shouted, '*Vel Akai, jook(Come here, dog!)*'" The *juckal* was off like a shot and he ran behind old Piramus at a gallop until they reached his camp at Romsey. There he stayed with old Piramus. The *jukal jinned(knew) that* he was back with his *foki(people)*."

After the visit to the hulks, Rebecca continued in her good spirits to Whitney's dismay. He watched as she drew closer and more motherly to Tom and Levi. It was as if she had changed into a totally different person. At times, it seemed that the boys were becoming her teacher. She would often go for walks in the forest with the boys and come back with bunches of wild flowers. He even overheard the boys teaching her Romany words. He was being driven to distraction by this sudden change in this woman that he deeply loved. He knew that he was losing her, so he mustered his courage and called her into his study for a last chance at reconciliation.

"Rebecca, I have watched you with admiration all of these years - how you have come down from your high position in society and done for those who are less fortunate. And I have ever always admired you for those very qualities. I don't think that I could ever find another woman to match my enthusiasm for charitable works. Would you please forgive me and give me another chance? We can be together in spirit for a few more years before we give ourselves to each other as man and wife."

"George, I love you and will always love you, but you are the sort of man who has to give yourself to a cause. I feel that I have given enough of myself to these causes. I know that you think I am selfish, but I hope that you will forgive me and not let it ruin our friendship, for my heart warms to another."

Whitney took a deep breath, he couldn't hide his anguish. Rebecca knew she was hurting him, but she had to let him know her true feelings. She couldn't look him directly in the eyes as she continued to pour out the last of her confessions. "One day Adam will be free and I know he is a man who will take me for his partner."

"Rebecca, he is a Gypsy. How could you marry him? You would live the life of a pariah. What would your father think?"

"I do not care what my father thinks. He will always hate and impose his views and one-sided justice on those around him. I cannot live for my father. And I've given all that I can to you and your mission. I need to have some personal joy and spiritual comfort and a life of my own. I've done enough for others and now I must do for myself.

"Spiritual comfort! You mean carnal pleasure! How could you even consider living the life of a Gypsy?"

"George, I'm sorry to have to say this to you but I am

in love with Adam. I love his children as if they were my own."

"Rebecca I am not a man who shows his emotions outwardly, if this is the way you feel, you must know that you have wounded my heart, but my feelings will always be steadfast towards you. I could not bear to see you in affectionate conversation with another man, so, I must tell you now that I cannot accompany you and the boys on any more visits with their father. Henceforth, you must find another to escort you and the boys to the hulks. I'm sure that their old uncle will be happy to take you. Now I must get back to my work."

# CHAPTER 9

The next night aboard the hulk, Hoskins sent a guard down below, to bring Adam to his quarters on the top deck. When Adam arrived, Hoskins invited him to sit at his table and he poured him a glass of rum.

"Five-One-Three, your time has come to pass muster. In a fortnight, several of the commanders of the hulks are going to gather in a field by Newport and bring their top men for a boxing match. The stakes are going to be high. Are you with me on this?"

"I'm game if there will be anything in it for me."

"You know that my word is good. Haven't I seen to it that you have a better place to sleep and better rations? Other prisoners have taken months, even years, to prove themselves well-disciplined enough to be moved to the higher decks with better mates."

"Yes you have, but if I am to do my best for you, then I would appreciate your assurance that I may have my sentence shortened."

"You do your best in this fight by finishing your man off neatly. In return, I will do my best to see that your stay here is not so permanent."

As the light of the candle lit both their faces, Adam looked into Hoskins watery eyes and saw honesty. He raised his cup. "To victory." Hoskin followed with, "And to your Freedom."

The sun sparkled on the waves of the solent. The convict oarsmen strained against the force of the bouncing water as they propelled the boat containing Hoskin's party towards the heavily populated spot on the shore of The Isle of Wight. The prisoners smiled like children on their way to a Sunday picnic, for this was not work for them. Today was a day for which they had waited months. They had watched their P's and Q's ever trying to appear to be the best and most deserving prisoners on the hulk to be given the honor of propelling Captain Hoskins' launch to this great sporting event. They may be chained at the ankle, but that would not prevent them from partaking in the food, drink and frivolity of the meeting. Of seeing and hearing the swells of London and men of every rank vying for and prophesying the winners of the matches and collecting big on their wagers.

This was a big deal to them. When they landed, soldiers helped them out and secured their boat. The whole party, including the prisoners, marched to their space beside of the quickly set-up rope ring.

"It's Gypsy Adam." Whispered a tall, thin fellow in a long drovers coat. "My money's on him."

His burly companion studied Adam's muscular frame, stroking his beard and nodding in agreement.

Jacques Rouseau had been brought along to serve as Adam's second. It was Adam's personal choice, for he knew of Jacques ability as a boxer and fierce combatant. Adam had bestowed the honor of water bottle carrier upon a young lad named Jeremy Wigglesworth. Adam felt sorry for him for bearing the burden of such a ridiculous surname. But he also admired him for his steadfast defense of his family name and honor, even coming to blows whenever the other prisoners made light of his name. When Adam first encountered the slight young man and had witnessed him being taunted and the ferocious manner in which he struck back at his tormentors, Adam took him aside and made him an honorary brother. "You know lad, when you are made fun of and laughed at because of your odd name, I feel your pain and frustration. This is the same pain I felt when people would call me 'filthy Gypsy.' But do you know what, little brother? I can never be ashamed of being a Gypsy, just as you can never be ashamed of being a Wigglesworth. Even the lowliest of paupers is no good to himself or his people if he is ashamed of himself. When men tried to belittle me by calling me a Gypsy, I told them: if you want to insult me, then call me what you are - a filthy gauja - and I will fight you."

Deeming Jeremy's surname too long to pronounce, Adam just called him "Wiggles."

The match was set and Adam entered the ring.

His opponent was a strapping giant. His name was Tom the Coalman because, before he was imprisoned for murdering a coal merchant, he had spent his youth shoveling coal in a Welsh coal mine. Tom discovered later that he could make more money extorting coal merchants and taking bribes to get well-paying coal haulers wagons to the front of the fill line by bruising and intimidating his way to the front. One unlucky day, he broke into the cue in front of an ex bare-knuckle boxer who had recently got a job as a coal hauler. The fight that ensued lasted for two hours.

Both men were beat beyond recognition. The honest coal hauler died shortly after the fight and Tom got a long sentence in the hulks.

Jacques and Jeremy followed Adam up to the ropes and stood by while Adam climbed into the ring to meet the referee and his opponent. Each man's hands and clothing were examined to make sure that they didn't contain any rocks, hard objects or substances like rosin to rub into the opponent's eyes. The referee then took a coin and asked Adam to call the toss. Adam obliged, "Heads, I say." The coin was flipped it came up tails, Jacques and Jeremy took their positions outside of Adam's undesirable corner. Tom the Coalman had won the coin toss and chose the best corner. Adam would now have to start each round with the bright sun glaring in his eyes.

The pugilist came to scratch, which was a mark made in the center of the turf boxing ring and there they stood toe to toe. The referee warned them, "I am here to see that you men fight like sports. If I see any serious fouls or dirty blows, then you will be disqualified and forfeit the fight. May God have mercy on your souls. Shake hands and come out fighting."

Adam turned his elbows down, raised his fists to face level, lowered his chin and danced his way towards the Coalman. As he came into his proximity, the Coalman grunted and launched several powerful punches at Adam's body. Adam weaved and bobbed, thrusting his torso backwards within a split second of each of the Coalman's blows which would have had a devastating effect on him had they landed. Before the Coalman could reset his balance, Adam stepped in and threw a powerful right-handed punch that contacted his jaw, shook his whole body and sent him reeling towards his corner. Cheers erupted from Adam's camp until the Coalman shook off the effects of the blow and quickly regained consciousness. The bell rang and the men retired to their prospective corners.

The second round started with several of The Coalman's disgruntled supporters shouting, "Kill the Gypsy!" These men had been drinking and had approached within the ten foot forbidden zone around the ring. The referee raised his hands and stopped the fight. He pointed at the hecklers and shouted, "If it's murder you are advocating gentlemen, please step up into the ring and insult this man to his face. If not, shut your cowardly mouths and go home and suck your Mum's bosom."

Laughter erupted ringside at the expense of the hecklers. They were taken in hand by the guards. Fight goers laughed at and taunted them as they were drug away through the crowd.

The commotion finally settled and the second round began. The Coalman charged around the ring following Adam who was much lighter on his feet. When Adam saw that the Coalman was tired, he stood his ground and the men exchanged a devastating flurry of blows. The exchange left both men with bruised and bloody faces. Adam was bleeding from a split lip. He had a bright red contusion on his forehead, but the Coalman got the worst of it. He had a large cut over his eye and blood streaming from a smashed nose.

The bell rang and Adam retired to his corner. Jacques swabbed the blood from his face with a wet cloth. Jeremy held the water bottle to his mouth and he took a long drink. "Mon ami, you are doing well, but you have to stay away from his punches. He is a powerful man. You must stay back and let him tire, just move in fast when you want to tap him and don't exchange with him again." Adam nodded, then Jacques took hold of his left hand and examined it. The cloth wraps across his  hand were split, The skin across his knuckles was torn open, exposing the white bone and gristle below. "Mon Dieu! You have damaged your hand on that bastard's ragged mouth. We must work fast." Jacques stood with his back concealing his actions from the opponent's corner. He took some strips of cloth and tightly wrapped Adam's injured knuckles. "Mon Ami, only one duke goes to battle, so, you must be careful."

Several rounds followed with neither man getting the upper hand. The Coalman realized that Adam was favoring his left hand and not throwing many punches with it. He began to work on Adam's left side, punching mostly with his right hand, even though he was left-handed. The Coalman was slowing down but he made a desperate and dangerous move on Adam in the ninth round, punching him in the kidney and groin. Adam doubled over in pain. He instinctively covered his crotch and turned away from The Coalman. As Adam fell to the ground, the Coalman continued to pound him on the back of his head. The referee pulled The Coalman away from Adam. "You have fouled out! go to your corner!" Jacques and Jeremy assisted Adam. He limped back to his corner in great pain. "Adam, are you alright?"

Adam winked at Jacques and gave him a weak smile. "He only ruptured one of me bollocks. I think I'll be alright, but let us see what the judge has to say."

The referee had called foul but the final say was with the judges who were seated with the commanding officers of the respective hulks. Hoskins approached Adam. "Can you continue the fight?" Adam looked at Hoskins in disbelief, then he stared towards his badly bruised adversary.

"Better than he?" Adam bounced and threw a couple of punches in the air to demonstrate that he still had fight in him.

"Legally the fight is forfeit and we are winners. But I must tell you that my greatest wager with the other commander was that you could last for ten rounds with his man. If they forfeit the fight now, then I will not collect on this bet. Are you willing to continue?"

"Yes, I will fight for you and I will win for you, but only if you promise me that I will be a free man in a year's time."

"Bless you, Five-One-Three. If you do this for me then you will have your wish, as well my gratitude."

Jacques patted Adam on the back as he prepared to go back to into ring, "Mon Ami, please make his jowls ring like the bells of Notre Dame for me."

"Oui Oui, Jacques!"

Adam headed out to the center of the ring and the Coalman faced off with him. The Coalman seemed distracted as he was looking towards his commanding officer and the judges. His captain shook his fist at him showing his displeasure at his performance. Now his attention was back on Adam. The Coalman tried his best to grapple with Adam and throw him down. Adam slipped and fell on the damp grass, but he rolled back up onto his feet before The Coalman could hammer him.

Adam continually peppered The Coalman during the round, delivering punches to his face and ribs. Adam caught his second wind. The Coalman tried but he couldn't connect any of his punches with the agile Adam.

The next time that the Coalman released his ponderous assortment of ill aimed punches, Adam warded them all off. When Adam saw that the winded Coalman was letting his guard down he went to work on him. He landed a heavy blow to his right side. The Coalman clenched his arm against his injured ribs. Adam attacked the Coalman's chin and jaw with a powerful one-two punch combination delivered within a split second. The Coalman's eyes rolled back in his head as his candles went out. He fell to the ground and stayed there. He was down for the count and Adam's supporters surrounded the ring with the continuously powerful chant of, "Gypsy!" "Gypsy!" "Gypsy!" But this time it was a positive statement of praise and it was music to Adam's ears.

# CHAPTER 10

Adam's last days in prison were his most miserable. The guards didn't like the fact that they were losing their favorite fighter, one who had filled their pockets from the wagers that they had made on him. But as Adam's release date neared, they all showed their respects by bringing him small gifts and token items.

As a smiling guard turned a key and Adam's cell door swung open, several of his cell mates began to clamor and cheer. The old hulk was reverberating with excitement by the time Adam reached the top deck.

With well wishers surrounding him Hoskins approached Adam, "I shall no longer call you Mr. Five-One-Three, Stanley, now that you are a free man." He handed Adam a packet. "My men have chipped in and purchased these gifts of tobacco and brandy for you. And I hope you will be willing to trade me that sturdy wool suit, those rusty chains and those old hobnail boots that you have been wearing these past years for this finely tailored suit and riding boots."

"Thank you, sir, but I hope that you know that I am

getting the better of the deal."

"Now you take this stuff and my good advice. I don't want to see your handsome face around these haunts ever again."

Adam smiled, reaching out his arms to accept the gifts from his once jailer now friend Hoskins.

Adam felt awkward receiving these gifts after being deprived of luxuries for such a long time. He placed his presents at his feet and he grabbed Hoskins hand and firmly shook it. At that moment Adam had another surprise, Reverend Whitney had just come aboard the hulk. "Mr. Whitney, sir, I am so happy to see you."

"Mr. Stanley, I want to make it clear to you that what ever has transpired between us and Rebecca, I still have my duty as a human being and a minister of God. I still am a friend and helper to you and your boys, so I will continue to try and right the wrongs that have been done to you."

Adam was overcome with emotion. He grabbed Whitney's hand. "Thank you, Reverend. Your being here for my release means a lot to me, for I am troubled and I wish to apologise for any hurt that I may have caused you."

Whitney smiled, "What can I say? Shall we leave it at that, brother? Let us just rejoice this blessed day."

Adam was curious, for it is the very first time that Whitney had come alone to the hulk. He instinctively turned and looked off into the distance to see that his boys and Rebecca were sitting in a carriage on the lane beside the Solent.

Adam was speechless. It humbled him to experience the humility and selflessness Whitney had shown by being here at this critical point in his life. "Mr. Whitney, thank you, dear sir, for all that you have done for me, though I am so undeserving of your charity. I am happy to see you, I am thankful that you have brought Tom and Levi to see me this day."

"What kind of parson would I be to not? I do only what I am easily capable of sir, and that is to show you that Jesus forgives those that forgive others, and to show you my true feelings towards you and your people."

"Thank you, sir, but I would not like for my boys or Miss Rebecca to see me in this filthy state of dress. Would you please take my clothing and gifts and meet me under yonder bridge?"

Adam pointed off in the distance to an old stone and wooden bridge.

Whitney answered, "Certainly." Adam handed him his package of clothing and gifts. Whitney bade farewell and was escorted down the stairway to a waiting launch for his short ride to shore.

After a blacksmith removed his leg chain, Adam made his way to the prow of the ship.

He ceremoniously removed each piece of his filthy stinking prison garb, cursed and spat on it, then threw it aside on the deck. Adam dove into the water of the Solent and swam fiercely away from the hulk.

As Adam swam with powerful strokes through the green frothy water of the Solent, his small party in the carriage watched his progress and followed slowly in the lane beside the water. Rebecca seemed confused by the chain of events. "What is he doing? Is he crazy? After all this and he is going to drown himself and leave these boys orphans?"

Whitney laughed, choosing this moment for a rare display of dry wit. "Rebecca, dear, you daresn't fret. Have you never seen a Gypsy at his toilet?" The boys laughed and Rebecca felt sheepish as they continued to follow Adam's progress towards the bridge.

Before Adam exited the water, he stood in the sandy shallows beneath the bridge. He grabbed handfuls of sand and scrubbed his body. He washed his face and stroked his hands through his thick black hair, trying to remove any traces of the prison filth,the odor or the vermin that had been part of his life for the last few years. He was not about to let Rebecca ever again see or smell the terrible *maukidiness*(impurity) that was part of him and his existence for this awful dark period of his life.

When Adam finished washing, he exited the water and waited under the bridge until Levi brought him his clothes and a small bottle of brandy. Levi handed his father his clothing, then, he turned and walked away to leave his father to dress in his sandy dressing room. Adam donned his clothing, rinsed his mouth with the brandy and climbed an embankment to the waiting arms of his family.

# Chapter 11

Adam spent several days near Southampton, happy to be with Rebecca and the boys. One day, Adam excused himself, "There is something that I must do. I have to find Uncle Wester." He told Rebecca.

"Well, if you must, then go then my love. I will wait for you. Please be careful." Adam borrowed a horse and rode through the forest near Beaulieu where he had heard that his Uncle Wester might be camped. Adam passed over a quaint bridge and into a secluded vale. There, just as he suspected, was his dear old uncle's camp. Uncle Wester was seated alone and contentedly weaving willow baskets. "Sar shan, how have you been my dear uncle?" Wester looked up at Adam as if he were an apparition,

"Is that you my boy? I heard that you was out of the *stariben(prison)*. *Dawdi*!(Lord!) What a blessing."

Adam gave his uncle an emotional embrace. "Uncle, do you still have what I left you to keep for me when I was taken up to the hulks?"

Uncle Wester hesitated momentarily, giving Adam a quizzical look. "What are you talking about, my boy?"

Adam studied Uncle Wester's puzzled expression. For a moment, he wondered if the old man may have lost his mind, and his life savings which he had entrusted to him when he was sent to prison. Uncle Wester, feeling the seriousness of the matter, leaves off his bad joke.

"Don't worry me *chavy*, I still got every bit of it, right here by your feet." Uncle Wester grabbed a shovel. Carefully he scraped the hot coals and ashes of the campfire aside. He then dug into the steaming blackened soil beneath where the fire had been. His shovel hit something hard. Removing the soil from around the object, Uncle Wester slid the shovel beneath a tarnished copper box which he lifted and set on the ground before Adam. Adam knelt down, touching the lid of the box. He seemed surprised as he addressed his uncle, "Just slightly warm."

Adam undid the clasp. He opened the lid of the box. He seemed relieved when he saw that his many pieces of fine family heirloom jewelry were present. He fingered the jewelry for a moment. Then, he pulled out an old leather pouch from a corner of the box. He untied the drawstring and emptied a pile of glistening gold sovereigns into his hand. "It's all here and you didn't spend a farthing of it." Adam took a few gold coins and he tried to put them into Uncle Wester's hand. Uncle Wester clinched his hand into a tight fist and he drew it away from Adam.

"Uncle, I remember when you used to put a silver shilling in your hand and challenge all the young men of the camp. If any one of them could open your fist then they could have it. No matter how hard they tried, none could ever pry or peel your fingers open enough to get it. Well, I'm trying to give you money this time and you are making it just as hard for me."

Adam finally gave up on his effort to repay Uncle

Wester for his loyalty. Uncle Wester looked Adam in the eye. "You've forgotten about your dear mother's George II silver tea service and silverware."

"No I haven't, uncle, I'm sure you have an explanation for where it's gotten to."

"Well, Adam, never fear. It's safe with your friend Isaac."

"You pawned it then, uncle?"

Uncle Wester smiled at Adam who could't hide his concern over what the pawn bill might be after his several years in prison.

"Nephew, that would have cost us dearly after all that time to get it back from storage. I made a special deal with him."

"What kind of deal did you make with Isaac?"

"One that I couldn't refuse. You see, he said he would keep it safe for you as long as you were in prison. But he also tried to buy it from me before that and at a quite a fair price for a shylock."

"Well, that makes me feel a site better. Thank you uncle - for what you've done for me."

"It weren't much, my boy, you'd have done it for me too, I know."

Adam took the jewelry and gold. He carefully placed it into his saddle bag. He hugged Uncle Wester farewell, furtively slipping several gold coins into one of Uncle Wester's broad coat pockets.

Adam rode back to Southampton, but this time he entered the commercial district and found the pawnshop of Isaac Goldschmidt, the Jewish money lender. Isaac had sympathy for the Gypsies, for his own people had suffered much in the same manner as the Gypsies from the persecution of the English hierarchy and judicial system. He also had an abiding hatred for Judge Kingsley who had caused not a few of his friends and family to suffer unjust imprisonment and executions for crimes of fencing and commerce which were laid at their doors by unscrupulous gentiles. Gentiles whose testimony always carried much more weight in court than did the often victimized Jew.

Isaac also happened to be a boxing promoter well-connected with the sporting crowd. Adam entered the pawnshop and greeted Isaac saying, "Old friend, would you know where a Gypsy bruiser might find himself a good match to fetch himself a few farthings?"

Isaac squinted and ran to the front of his shop, "Adam, brother, I have been waiting for you since word reached me of your release. I suppose you didn't just come here to see my lovely face?"

"Isaac, yes I did. It will always be lovely to me, but my Uncle Sylvester said that you were keeping something for me." Adam handed Isaac a worn and barely legible pawn ticket. Isaac took the ticket and he squinted his eyes to read it.

"Yes I am. It is quite a lovely service and it will break my dear wife's heart when I have to give it back. You see, I have not been storing it in a dusty store room. My wife would not have it. She took her best dishes from our glass front dining room cabinet and placed your tea service in it. She has turned every Jewess in the south of England green with envy by flashing that teapot."

"Well Isaac, uncle told me of your terms and I much appreciate your kindness. I am not ready to take the silver out of pawn yet, so please, by all means, charge me for your services."

"My friend, you are doing me a favor by letting us keep the silver, and boosting Sarah's status among her friends for having it to show."

"There is one more thing. I have some other pieces of silver and jewelry that I would like to pawn. I need the funds to prepare for my wedding."

"Adam, splendid. I'm your man, on the condition that I'm invited and preferably as your groomsman."

"That, my dear Isaac, will depend on how generous your terms are."

"Ha Ha Ha! The hulks didn't dampen your wit. You're still my Gypsy Adam!"

Adam pawned the jewelry and silver, happy to have reconnected with his old friend Isaac.

Isaac was a shrewd dealer. He knew the financial health of most of the prominent families in England. He also knew which family was having problems from the information he gathered from his network of friends and family in the pawn business. He knew what husband was pawning his wife's jewelry or what gambling addict was laying his family's fortunes to waste.

In England, Isaac saw first-hand how the rich mill owners worked small children for long hours on low pay to support their lifestyles. As a business money lender, he traveled to coal mines in the north of England where he saw women and children working deep underground. They were struggling to push and pull heavy coal wagons up out of the dark mine shafts. Isaac was not shy about registering his disgust of this inhumane business practice, even though his sharp complaints greatly displeased his prospective loan seekers.

Isaac knew well these men who ran the mines in England. He also knew that they were worried about losing their unethical supply of cheap labor. Children from the families of workhouse inmates and orphans. Church leaders and politicians were raising their voices against these brutal child labor practices. These mine operations would one day soon need a new means of pulling these mine carts from hell, so Isaac set his plan in motion.

Isaac started going to horse fairs, buying up all the small-breed horses and ponies he could find. Shetland, Exmoor and New Forest ponies fit the bill. The Gypsy horse traders didn't miss this new player on the scene. Uncle Wester and Levi took Isaac aside and made a proposition to supply him with all of the New Forest ponies he could handle. They would break and train them for an additional fee. Soon a cartel was formed between the New Forest Gypsies and Isaac. Isaac became the go-to supplier to the British mining industry due to his Gypsy horse trading contacts.

Things went well at first, but many of the mine owners were reluctant to give up their old ways and cheap labor. Isaac had made it clear to loan seekers that he would not garner loans for any mine owner that used girls or children in their operations. He even went so far as to supply draft animals and harnesses for a year with no interest on payments to implement his improvement of child welfare.

Isaac was born in Romania and he had remained in contact with his relatives in Eastern Europe. He heard from them about the ups and downs in the commodity and industrial markets. He read newspapers from the continent, so he knew that times were about to change for the underdog.

Isaac also had read about the French Enlightenment and how it was spreading among the Romanian intelligentsia. There were calls for the abolishment of Gypsy slavery in Romania, Isaac knew that Gypsy slaves supplied the might and muscle to keep the Romanian mines working. So, his future plans included creating a market for small draft horses that could be used as compact draft animals to replace Gypsy slave labor in the mines of his birth country Romania.

One day, Isaac ran into Adam at a livery stable where Adam was delivering a horse for sale. "Fine piece of horseflesh." Isaac couldn't resist examining the horses mouth. "Can't be a day over three years old?"

"Try ten, this horse is a masterpiece of the jockey's art." Isaac took another walk around the beautiful chestnut colored stallion. "So, my friend has taken the wrong path again?"

"Not at all. I just took this horse in on a debt owed me by one of my people. John the liveryman here knows perfectly well the history of this horse. He sold it to a Gypsy several months ago. If anyone is duped here, then it won't be a Gypsy doing the duping. We don't hold the position as the only underhanded dealers in England."

"Well, is the wedding day set then?"

"I'm not quite ready Isaac, but by the way business is going, a month or so may get me on my feet enough to pay the bill. You know that when we throw a party it is for the whole village and we don't spare the drink."

# Chapter 12

Time was growing short and Rebbeca had been pro-
crastinating. Finally, she summoned up enough nerve
to venture back to her father's house and gather the things
that she needed to prepare for her wedding. Aunt Betty
saw Rebecca getting into her carriage. "Rebecca, where
are you going?"

"I must go home to Father and tell him of my plans to
marry, and gather what little I have left in his house before
he hears the news from others."

"Well let me accompany you, or at least drive for you."

"No, Aunt Betty. Thank you for the kind offer, but this
is the one time that my homecoming will be much more
painful than my leaving."

Upon her arrival Rebecca was greeted by Kingsley's
chief keeper Williams. "Miss Rebecca, so nice to see you
again."

"Thank you, Mr. Williams. Could you see to it that my
horse is watered?"

"Certainly, Miss Rebecca. It will be a pleasure."

As Rebecca was helped from her carriage, she spoke.

" Mr. Williams, I would like to invite you to a wedding."

"Why thank you Miss, and I assume that it will be yours?"

"Yes, and please bring the wife. There will be plenty of food, drink and dancing. It will be at Fareham, first Saturday in June."

"If the judge will give me leave then I most definitely will be there. Much obliged for your kindness, Miss."

"And Mr. Williams, please extend the invitation to your friend John."

"For sure, Miss, that I will. Oh, you will find your father busy in his study. He gave orders for us servants not to bother him on any account, but I will make sure he is told that you are here to see him."

"Thank you, Mr. Williams."

Rebecca was led into the great receiving hall of her old home. She sat on what was once her mother's favorite chair. It still bore the deep scratch in the enamel paint across the arm that Rebecca had made with a pair of scissors while sitting in her mother's lap while she was embroidering. A tear trickled down Rebecca's cheek as memory and tactile feel melded together to bring back thoughts of that long ago incident. An incident which drew her father's rage and her mother's equally powerful outrage at his overreaction to her innocent childhood accident. The memory of the sound of her father's angry voice faded for a moment. But momentarily, Rebecca was shocked back into reality by a loud disturbance in a distant part of the house.

Williams had delivered the news of her return and Judge Kingsley reacted to Williams' intrusion.

"Rebecca! Rebecca! What does she want?"

"Sir, she wishes to see her Father, if that what you be."

"If that what I be? If that what I be? Of all the insulant remarks with which a servant could address his master, I have a notion to thrash you right now. But I will refrain, because Mr. Williams you are absolutely right. But I will have to correct you, because your English is atrocious. Your impertinent outburst should have been, not , 'If that what you be,' but, 'If that is what you are.'"

Rebecca stood and turned and, to her surprise, she was greeted by her father. "Rebecca, I am sorry for raising my voice and telling you that you are not welcome in our house."

"I too am sorry, Father. I'm sorry that you took what I said as disrespect, but that is the past and now is a new day. I have come to gather some clothing and sundry items from my room, if you will permit me."

"Of course daughter, what's yours is yours."

"Thank you, Father, I shan't take long."

"Take as long as you like, Rebecca. Your presence is like a breath of fresh air to this old place."

Rebecca smiled and placed her hand on her father's face. The tension was now broken, her father embraced her. Then, she turned and made her way up the stairs to her room. She opened a cedar trunk and took from it a delicate heirloom wedding dress and held it up to her body. It conformed perfectly to her shape. It had been her mother's. She knew from experience to not let her father see it, for it would be very upsetting to him. It had once been pearly white when Rebecca was a little girl and she dreamed of wearing it in her own wedding to a handsome prince. But the years had changed it to a not unpleasant vanilla color.

Rebecca took the dress, folded it and placed it in a leather valese. She picked a flattering bonnet from her wardrobe and some ribbons from her stock to match. As she made her way down the stairs, she felt an empty feeling in the pit of her stomach and tears began to flow from her eyes. She knew that she had to be honest with her father and tell him of her impending marriage to Adam. She knew that it would be a shock, and so she prepared herself for what she knew would be an emotional maelstrom.

Her father was waiting for her when she reached the bottom of the stairway. "Daughter, will you have some tea with me?"

"Thank you, Father, of course I will."

She walked into the kitchen and father and daughter sat down at a small table. Rebecca sat her valese on the floor by her side. Her father poured her a cup of tea and offered her a small plate of shortbread. Rebecca drank her tea and enjoyed the sweet shortbreads.

"And how are things at the mission?"

"Everything is going well, Father. I am to be married next month."

"What? Well, that is wonderful. You must give my congratulations to Reverend Whitney. Please tell him that henceforth my house is open to you both, and if you wish, you can have your wedding party here."

"Father, I am not marrying George."

"What? Not George? What of your engagement?"

"Broken a year hence, George would never marry me until he had reached his goals of establishing his several missions for the poor."

"Well then Rebecca, who is the luckey man?"

"You will not like to hear it, Father, for I am to wed Adam Stanley."

"What? That Gypsy pugilist! Have you lost all reason,

Rebecca?"

"No, I love him and his sons who I have fostered these last years."

"My God, Rebecca, how could you lower yourself to sully your person and reputation by consorting with such a common criminal and Gypsy."

"He is not a criminal. You and your court unjustly imprisoned him. Your greedy bailiffs killed his wife and ripped him away from his children."

"He was duly tried and convicted. He paid the price for his transgressions."

"There was no theft of horses, Father. Adam was totally innocent of his brother's crime of paying too little for a rich man's hobby horses sold by the man's own kin."

"That is not the issue. He knew of his brother's crime and he did not report it."

"Would you go to a hostile institution that was the bane of your existence and sign your own brother's death warrant? Just because he had the bad judgement of dealing with uscrupulous gentry who were selling horses at a ridiculous price so that a debt collector could not profit from them?"

"That is not the point, Rebecca. You will never understand my motives, and why I can only deal with this type of people in an unbending way."

"No, Father. I don't think that I will ever understand your hate for the less fortunate members of society and whatever motives you might use to justify it."

"Rebecca, I have suffered a great wrong and your mother has suffered a great wrong. I can not say more, I promised her and she made me swear an oath that I would never burden you with our sorrows. I cannot say more now, but one day maybe before I die you will know my reasons."

"I will not venture to guess your reasons father, but I neither expect, nor need your approval, to marry Adam. You are responsible for the loss of a man's wife and the disruption of his family. How poetically just it will be for you to replace his dead wife with your own daughter. The Lord works in strange ways, does he not Father?"

"Rebecca, don't do this."

"Father, I love you but I cannot obey you nor forgive you for what you have done to bring suffering to the families of unfortunate souls who have had the misfortune to come under your vindictive judgement."

"My daughter, if you dare follow through with this travesty then you are not welcome in this house. I will see to it that your Gypsy never touches a farthing of Kingsley property."

Rebecca turned and walked away from her father without uttering a word. With the help of a servant, she carried her clothing and possessions out to her carriage. As she climbed into the carriage, she tried to conceal her tears from the servant.

"Miss, is everything alright?" Rebecca forced a smile.

"Oh everything is fine, now."

Weeks had passed and preparations were well underway for the wedding. Judge Kingsley had been miserable for the whole month since learning of Rebecca's plans. As he sat in his parlor, nervously reading the newspaper announcement of the Gypsy wedding and reception at the Fareham Mission, a maid approached. "Sir, your man Williams would like to talk to you."

Kingsley folded the newspaper and placed it so that the wedding announcement was hidden from view, as if he were ashamed for his servant to see it. Williams toddled in with his cap in his hand and a nervous look on his face. "Sir, I have a request to make."

"Go ahead man, speak up."

"Well sir, my wife has boughten material and made a nice dress for herself and a shirt for yours truly."

"Yes man, come on Williams, finish your story."

"Sir, I would be forever indebted to you if you were to give me next Saturday off to attend church."

"Williams, isn't attending Sunday service sufficient to pay your religious obligations?"

"Well, sir, about the new clothes - they are for a party and the wife has her heart set on it."

"A party? what kind of party?"

"Well, sir, you see, at this party they are having a roasted ox, and beer and cider by the barrel."

"Come now, Williams, you are not telling me that you are willing to betray your master by going to that Gypsy's and my profligate daughter's wedding?"

"Well sir, I do feel right bad about it but the wife and children have set high hopes for me to bring them there."

"What of your mate John? I suppose he would like to turn traitor on me also."

"No, sir. John has no intention on going."

"I don't believe you. Go bring John to me. I think you are a cunning liar. I want to hear it from his own lips."

Williams left to room and Kingsley addressed his maid. "Humph, Constance I cannot believe that the glutton of Hampshire has no interest in attending an ox roast."

The maid smiled politely, amused at Kingsley's rare expression of humor and pleased at his addressing her by her name.

Shortly thereafter, Williams and John entered the parlor. Both were in a state of apprehension as these kinds of meeting were always a time for the judge to vent his frustrations with mistakes they had made in the performance of their duties. Kingsley rose from his chair and spoke. "John, Williams here has asked me my leave to allow him to go to the Gypsy's wedding this Saturday. What say you to this?"

"Well, apologizing to you for your displeasure with Miss Rebecca, sir. But I think you should let the good man go."

"You do?"

"Yes sir, I do."

"Now I don't suppose that you have any fancies about feeding upon steak, drinking your fill of cider and beer and tapping your foot to fiddle music, do you?"

"No sir, I'd be obliged to stay and work and serve you if it be agreeable to you."

"Oh, that would be very agreeable to me, but for the fact your words do not ring true. I have not sat on the judicial bench for thirty years for no reason. I know a bald faced lie when I hear one. Now be honest with me, man."

Williams stepped forward. "Sir, John here is deathly afraid of the Gypsy. He fears being seen by him at the wedding."

"Why would that be?"

"Well, sir, when you sent us out to shift the Gypsy off of your estate, The Gypsy gave John a real facer."

John placed his hand on his neck. "And I ain't been the same ever since. I been dizzy and I got a wry neck."

"Fools! Why did you not report the assault? I would have had the miscreant arrested for that."

"It weren't the Gypsy's fault, sir, John was breaking the tent down on top of his wife and child."

John interrupts. "I thought about it for a long while sir

and I didn't tell you because the man was only protecting his family from harm."

"John, you have a softer heart than I, but it is you who must live with the injuries. So, I can't punish a man for his good nature. Williams, I give you permission to go to the wedding. John, if you are inclined, then you may have leave too. At least I can benefit from you two filling your guts at the expense of the Gypsy and not from my pantry."

# Chapter 13

In a back room of the Fareham rectory, Aunt Betty fussed with the ribbons on Rebecca's bonnet. Her mother's pretty wedding dress had been carefully cleaned and freshened to smell like a floral boquet. Rebecca was a picture perfect image of a wholesome English country bride with her glossy flowing hair and her rosy cheeks.

It was near noon and Adam had been spending his last moments of being a widower with his friends at the Black Boar Inn. He was dressed in the fine brown suit and riding boots that Commander Hopkins of the hulks had given him, with the addition of a fine beaver top hat and a gold handled walking cane. Uncle Wester ordered a round of the *cushtiest tattapanni*(best liquor)in the house and raised his glass to Adam. "To my nephew, Adam, a son I never had, a *tatchi moush*, a *tatchi dadus*, and a *tatchi Romnichel - Cousta bok* and a *coushti meripen*.( To a real man, a real father, and a real Gypsy - good luck and a good life)."

The crowd cheered the toast with "Here!, here!" Then, loud applause. After the noise subsided and the drinks were finished, the wedding party left the tavern and the men made their way down the lane to the mission chapel.

Adam met a gaggle of Romnichel boys near the mission, among whom his well-dressed sons Levi and Tom were playing. He grabbed their hands and they all walked into church. They were greeted by Reverend Whitney. They shook hands and Whitney motioned for Adam to follow him into the vestibule. "Mr. Stanley, I know that you might think it strange that I would be not only willing, but also demanding that I be the person to perform this wedding ceremony."

Adam felt ashamed of what he had done to Whitney, but he tried not to reveal his feelings. "I would think it strange sir, if it were any other man but you. I have the greatest respect for you Reverend, but right now I must confess that I feel as small as a mouse, and as low as the heel of your shoe for what I have done to you."

"Cheer up Mr. Stanley, no reason for guilt. I love Rebecca every bit as much as you do. I will always wish and pray for her happiness in this life. I have found that I was not capable of making her happy. And for whatever reason you are. So, I want to be here for her from the start of her new life with you. My great sacrifice of the love of my life will be my wedding gift to you. I hope you appreciate it and always honor and value her as much as I do. My having animosity towards you and her would only destroy me. So, let us begin."

Adam had never had so many mixed emotions flowing through his mind. He thought how can this be one of the happiest days of his life, and yet also one of the saddest. He felt sad for Reverend Whitney, a man whose goodness had rescued him from his blackest days by helping him preserve his family and also his will to live. And now this man was relinquishing the love of his life to him and absolving him of guilt while blessing his marriage to Rebecca.

The church was full of the mission staff, friends of Rebecca and Adam, and, of course, Aunt Richanda and Uncle Wester who were in the front pew. They were dressed in attire befitting a rustic lord and lady, but strangely Richanda held by her side a strange long thin item wrapped in cloth. She was asked by an usher if she would like him to store it for her, but she vehemently refused and held onto it all through the service.

When Whitney first saw Rebecca, he smiled and thought how lovely she looked at that moment. A tear slid from the corner of his eye and he turned around momentarily to hide this evidence of sorrow. He again faced the couple while making a point to smile at Adam to hide the fact that his heart was breaking.

Whitney began, "Dearly beloved, we are gathered together here in the sight of God, and in the face of this congregation, to join this man and this woman in holy matrimony." He continued with fervor and conviction to pronounce from memory each and every line unabridged from the wedding ceremony of the Book of Common Prayer. When he finished the vows, the wedding guests applauded not only the participants but the end of the long tedious service. The loud applause startled Uncle Wester who had fallen asleep. Maybe the drawn out wedding ceremony was a way to force penance on Adam and Rebecca for the pain that they had caused him. If it was, neither one could begrudge him of this right.

The vows completed, Adam placed the wedding ring on Rebecca's finger and then he kissed the bride. Rebecca hugged Whitney for a long moment and kissed him on his cheek. Adam shook Whitney's hand and held his shoulders at arms length, looking into his eyes he addressed him. "Thank you. No words can express the feeling of humility that I feel standing before your greatness and kindness. Reverend, I owe you more than any man can owe another."

"Just treat her the way that she deserves to be treated. I envy you, Adam, but I bless this union, and I wish you and Rebecca eternal happiness."

"Wait! Wait! Everyone, don't move!" Aunt Richanda shouted as she rose from the front pew. Unwrapping the strange bundle, she produced a new broom decorated with ribbons and flowers. She walked up to the couple and laid the broom across the aisle. "And now my dears, you cannot be a proper Romnichel couple until you jump the broom together as all our foki from times of old have have done." Aunt Richanda clapped her hands, the mission doors opened, and as planned two fiddlers began to play a wedding jig. Rebecca was totally surprised, but game to follow Adam's lead. He grabbed her hand and they both jumped over the broom. They walked hand in hand past their guests looking straight ahead until they exited the church as was the old custom.

Everyone was in great spirits as they left the church. Adam and Rebecca led them to the center of the mission campus where portions of roast oxen were being cut up and placed in large pans set beside loaves of fresh baked bread. Every plate in the mission was brought out and loaded with meat, bread and potatoes. Adam and Rebecca walked around and shared small talk with their guests, making sure that everyone felt well accommodated. Adam saw that Uncle Wester was busy in the corner drinking beer and chatting with his friend The Colonel. As he turned to greet another local, he saw the broad backs of two familiar men seated at a table. It was Kingley's keepers Williams and John, and they were too busy wolfing down roast ox to notice him. Adam walked up to them and clasped his hand on John's shoulder. "You enjoying the beef?"

John slowly turned his sore neck to see Adam's smiling face. His mouth was full of bread and meat. He tried to swallow and speak but only choked a bit in the process. Williams answered for him. "Excellent, Sir. Thanks for your indulgence, royal beef from a royal host."

"Good, good. I want to thank you both for coming, and I hope that you enjoy yourselves." Adam reached out his hand and Williams promptly shook it. He offered his hand to John who hurriedly wiped his greasy fingers on his trouser leg then he shook it.

"No hard feelings, men. I hope that we can be friends from this day forward."

Williams answered while the dumbfounded John nodded in agreement. "Thank you, sir. Bless you and Miss Rebecca, er Mrs. Stanley, and God Bless your marriage."

"Thank you, and don't forget the beer and cider. There's plenty to go around."

After talking to Kingsley's men, Adam saw Uncle Wester walking aimlessly around the grounds carrying a large mug of beer. "Uncle, how do you like the party?"

"Oh, it's good, good, but where does a man get a bite to eat?"

"You haven't eaten?"

"*No, the gaujas* are so thick and busy around the *hobben(food)* that I can't get a bit of meat and bread. And where is the *bauler(pig)*? T'ain't a real Romnichel wedding without *baulo mass(pig meat)*."

"Uncle, the ox is for the *gaujas*. The real wedding feast

is in the garden behind the rectory."

"Well why didn't you say so?"

"Because you were to busy talking to the Colonel and drinking beer. Now go through the garden gate and you will find a long table covered with luscious vittles and suckling pig, and a great wedding cake filled with fruits, sweatmeats and rum."

Uncle Wester still held onto his ruffled feather attitude as he walked past Kingley's keepers he gave them a disdainful look. "*Suv these gaujas*(frig these non gypsies)." He walked on with an aire of aloofness towards the rectory. Uncle Wester joined the family wedding party. He was seated and served regally like a guest of honor.

After everyone in the garden has had their fill, a toast was made to the bride and groom and the wedding party joined the village guests in drinking and dancing to the fiddlers tunes. After a while, Uncle Wester stood up from the table, lit his pipe and joined in the merriment. Adam approached him, "Uncle, where is Aunt Richanda?"

"She is back at the garden, she won't come out. I tried to make her but she won't join the party."

Adam opened the gate and walked into the garden area to see Aunt Richanda sitting by herself drinking beer and tapping her foot to the music. "Aunt, come join the party and dance with your nephew."

"*Kekker chor(no boy)*, I can't mix with that crowd."

"Why not?"

"I tried, but everytime I took three steps out of the yard, a *mauta gauja juvel*(drunk non gypsy woman) would grab me and try to *chiv vonger* in my *vast*(put money in my hand)."

"Is that so?"

"Yeah, I done *dukkered*(told fortunes to) half of them

before and they won't let me be. The silly *juvals*(women) are all so up with the cider and beer that they all think that they are Cinderreli at the ball, out to get themselves a handsome prince. *Dawdi*! I won't get a minutes peace if I show my face. I'm having a good time just sitting here drinking my bit of beer and watching the *foki*. Go on, nephew, I'll be just fine."

Adam hugged his aunt and smiled at her. He heard her sing a little drunken ditty as he walked to the gate. "Oh deary me, Oh deary me, what *dinelos(fools)* these *gaujas* be."

# Chapter 14

Adam had realised long before Rebecca's wedding day that she was a highborn woman who had been raised with servants and every advantage. Despite the fact that she had taken up a spartan lifestyle as an adult, which was part of serving the poor and destitute at the mission. Therefore, she would have a hard time adjusting to the Romnichel lifestyle. Adam could not see Rebecca squatting to enter a smokey bender tent and being happy to nurse her children on a bed of straw, so he bought her a cottage near the mission. Though not pretentious, it sat on a nice-sized lot with a garden and a clearing that stretched back into a beautiful green wood. Best of all, the cottage was distant from neighbors so Adam could invite Uncle Wester or any of his Romnichel relatives to camp on his land without problems from intrusive or complaining neighbors.

Adam had kept the cottage a secret from Rebecca, but he also had a beautiful *Vardo* (living wagon) built for her by a great wagonmaker who had built them for wealthy circus and fun fair owners. It was covered with colorful carvings, scrollwork and sported etched glass windows. Inside it had a comfortable bed, a dry sink, cabinets, and a little cast iron stove. Aunt Richanda had taken it upon herself to supply the interior decorations, bedding and curtains so that it would be a proper Romany Vardo.

The wagon had been set back in the clearing behind the cottage to serve as a honeymoon retreat. To make the camp inviting, Adam had also set up a bender tent complete with straw and bedding. He made sure that there was a nice fire going and a pot hook to hold cooking utensiles. Aunt Richanda had just placed a wicker basket filled with dining ware, beverages and good food beneath the wagon for Adam and Rebecca's honeymoon.

It was afternoon and the party was nearly over. Men and women of the village, along with local farm people, came up to Adam and Rebecca. They all thanked Adam and Rebecca for the wonderful hospitality that they had been shown. "Sir, we have never been so well treated by a host, and never with such good taste and food and drink and with such generosity."

Adam answered, "I want to thank all of you good people for coming and bringing such good feeling and joy to my wedding. I am happy and honored to have well wishers and neighbors such as you." Adam said his goodbyes to everyone including Tom and Levi, to whom he gave orders. "Miss Rebecca and I are going away for a few days, so I want you boys to be especially well-behaved. Now listen to Aunt Betty, as well as your aunt and uncle."

Levi spoke "We will, dad, we are so happy for you and Miss Rebecca. Can we give her a kiss before she goes?"

"Of course you can Levi, you should never again ask me such a question. Rebecca is now your mother."

Levi and Tom both hugged Rebecca and kissed her on

her cheek. Tom lisped, "Miss Rebecca, me and Levi are happy to have such a beautiful n' good mother."

"I'm happy to have such handsome and good boys."

Uncle Wester arrived with a carriage all decked out in ribbons and frills. The newlyweds climbed inside. Rebecca looked at Adam. "Where are we going? Far Away?" "Yes, very far away to an exotic place. In fact I'm taking you to a caravan."

"A caravan. Adam, I was not prepared for that kind of journey. Do we have to go?"

"Yes, dear, we must."

"But Adam, how long will we be gone?"

"Oh, a day or two."

"Please don't trifle with me, Adam. Where is this caravan?"

"Deep in the forest. Just around the next bend in the lane."

Rebecca slapped Adam's shoulder. "What are we doing, Adam?"

"Just wait."

Uncle Wester left the lane and drove back behind the cottage to the Gypsy camp in the clearing. "So, this is your caravan, Adam?"

"No, it's our caravan, and your new home."

"And for whom is the tent?"

"For my sons, of course."

"Oh, I see. Well, let's have a look."

Rebecca climbed up into the Vardo wagon and sat on the bed. "Very nice, in fact more than nice. I actually thought that you might expect me to live in a tent with you, which I would have. But yes, I think I could enjoy living with you in this little bird's nest."

Uncle Wester stuck his face through the wagon door

and took a look around. "Adam, nephew, I think you got something here. This is a real *kuver* (thing). It'll beat the hell out of sleeping on the ground in a tent. Especially for a man like me with rheumatism and all. I'd love to get one for the aunt and me. So this is where she's been. I thought that she done went *divia*(mad), telling me that she was decorating a wagon for you. Yeah, I think that this is the future for us Romnichels. I'll give the tent to me *jukels*."

"Glad you like it, uncle. I'll see to it that you get one too."

"Thanks, nephew. Now I'll leave you two lovebirds alone in your gilded nest."

Rebecca and Adam put their bags into the vardo and then they walked around the camp. Adam took the kettle and they walked hand and hand back into the woods.

"This place is so beautiful, Adam. How well do you know the cottagers?"

"Oh, I know them very well. In fact, they said that we can stay here as long as we like."

"They must be very nice people. I would like to meet them."

"You will very soon, but I'd like you to see their spring. It has the sweetest water."

They walked to the base of a small hill where the spring issued out of a rocky pit. Rebecca knelt down, dipped her hands in and tasted it.

"Oh, it is so cold. It is sweet and refreshing. It should make good tea."

Adam filled the pot, and the couple walked back to the camp. The sun was getting lower and was just peeping through the tree tops in the distance. Adam put the kettle on the fire to boil and Rebecca set up a small camp table and chairs. Adam found the large wicker chest beneath the vardo and carried it over so that they could see what Aunt Betty and Aunt Richanda had packed for them.

"Look dear, Aunt Betty has packed some of her delicious scones and strawberry marmalade. Aunt Richanda has packed us some of her wonderful rice pudding. And look, there is some red wine and a nice bottle of brandy. That must be from Uncle Wester."

Rebecca and Adam enjoyed their private tea and desserts. They drank the wine and sampled the brandy and conversed. As the veil of evening came down and the alcohol began to take effect, they both came to the realization that it was the very first time that they had been alone together.

"Adam, I feel a little uncomfortable asking you this, but, would you kiss me?"

As the last word passed Rebecca's lips, Adam silently answered her request and they kissed for long moments standing before the fire. Adam took her hand and led her into the tent. They took off their shoes and sat for a while on the woolen coverlet, staring into the fire.

Adam spoke, "Rebecca, in jest I told my French friend Jacques, in prison, that one day I would make you my wife. He laughed at me and said, 'I have just been told the greatest fairytale that I have ever heard.'"

"Don't feel guilty, Adam. I felt the same way about you from the moment that I set eyes on you. Now both our fairytales have come true." They spent most of the evening in the tent, but when the fire died down and a light chill came through the air, the couple took a candle and made their way to the comfort of their cozy caravan.

In the morning, Rebecca awoke to see prisms of light playing on the wooden floor of the caravan, produced from the bright morning sunshine coming through the etched glass windows. She stretched and rolled over and hugged the strong tawny back of her new husband. "Adam, Aunt Betty put some eggs and bacon and a nice loaf of bread in the basket for our breakfast."

"Oh dear, a newlywed like yourself shouldn't have to cook. What if I were to request a sumptuous breakfast for us from the cottagers?"

"I would think that rather rude of you Adam, just to presume to impose on such nice a people who would allow us, Gypsies that we are, to camp in such a beautiful place."

"Get dressed, dear. Let us make ourselves presentable and we shall see who is right."

Adam and Rebecca washed themselves in a basin of springwater and put on some comfortable clothing. Adam lifted the wicker basket containing the food and dining items. They both began the walk of several hundred yards up to the cottage. Rebecca became apprehensive as they neared the cabin, she knew from experience that most gaujas wanted nothing to do with Gypsies and now that she was a gypsy by marriage, this odium fell on her head. She didn't like the idea that her husband was pushing his luck with what she percieved to be very nice gaujas.

"Adam, are you sure that you want to impose on these people to cook for us? I would love to do it."

"These people are simpletons dear - pushovers, just you wait and see."

Adam walked up to the door and set the basket down. He looked at the nervous face of Rebecca and continued his charade as he knocked loudly on the door. To Rebecca's surprise, a smiling, familiar face answered the door. It was Aunt Betty. "Come in, come in, the breakfast is ready."

Rebecca was dumfounded. She was also greeted by

Tom, Levi, Aunt Richanda and Uncle Wester as she entered the cabin. "What's this? What a surprise. Where are the cottagers?"

Adam held Rebecca's shoulders and spoke directly to her. "We are the cottagers, dear. This is our home. Last night you spent your first night in a Gypsy tent and tonight I shall spend my first night in a *gauja* house."

# Chapter 15

Rebecca and Adam adjusted well to cottage life. Rebecca still offered her services to the mission, while The boys spent a lot more time with Uncle Wester and their father, learning the skills they needed to become successful Romnichel. Adam, knowing how much Uncle Wester loved the fancy *vardo*, gave it to him for he and Aunt Richanda to live in, so long as they stayed on his property or nearby. He knew that it would be healthier for them, and they were such good help with the boys. But the real reason was that their being around made life a hell of a lot more interesting.

Tom and Levi, being the boys that they were, decided to make the bender tent their home. The first night that they attempted to spend in it didn't work out too well. They came prepared with a dark lantern loaned to them by Uncle Wester. It was made of tin and had a sliding shutter that could be used to hide the candle flame inside. Uncle Wester had used it in his poaching days to slip through the woods without attracting the attention of the gamekeepers. The light that it emitted was feeble and with the breeze it danced and flickered and blew out. So, the boys just decided to lie down and go to sleep. Sleep didn't come easy, for the night was full of the sounds of the forest. An owl sat on a dead tree at the edge of the forest and began to hoot. "What's that, Levi?"

"That's just an old *mulo*(ghost) Tommy, trying to find his way back to the church yard."

"Let's go home, Levi. I don't want to stay out here."

*"You* ain't got nothing to be *trashered* (afraid)of Tom, ghosts can't hurt you none. It's the old Beng(devil) that you got to worry about."

"Levi, let's *lel*(get) our *koppers*(blankets)and *jall*(go) back to the *kair*(house)."

"How about me telling you a *coushta mulo*(good ghost) story?"

"No,--- What's that noise?" The boys became quiet. They listened and heard a rustling in the dry sticks and leaves behind their tent. Then came the mournful sound of a caterwauling female cat and the unnerving cries of her tomcat suitors as they fought and clawed for the right to breed with her.

Levi and Tom wasted no time in gathering their blankets and making their way back to the safety of their warm cottage.

Tom and Levi tried to camp out more as they got older. Now as big boys, they were ashamed of admitting that they were afraid to sleep out. If they were ever startled again, they stopped running back to their cottage. Instead, they knocked on Uncle Wester's door and he let them save face by allowing them to sleep on the floor of the vardo.

More and more now, Levi and Tom accompanied Adam on jaunts to buy, sell and trade horses. When horse fairs were held Adam borrowed the vardo from Uncle

Wester. He would take Rebecca and the boys, along with a string of horses, and make his way to the fair. Adam would meet old friends and relatives at the horse fair, while catching up on the gossip and news of the Romany world. On these occasions, Uncle Wester and Aunt Richanda would move into the little bender tent and Uncle Wester would joke about it being his second honeymoon, to Aunt Richanda's chagrin.

# Chapter 16

Christmas was a joyous time for the Stanley family. There were presents all around. Adam saw to it that every child at the mission had a new set of clothes and a warm winter coat. There was caroling led by Rebecca, and Tom and Levi joined the group as they went from house to house in the neighborhood. Of all the surprises of the holiday season, the biggest one was the announcement by Rebecca that she was expecting.

Spring arrived and Rebecca wasn't able to perform her duties at the mission because she had a problem plagued pregnancy. Her doctor ordered her not to exert herself, and to stay off of her feet. Adam was staying with her and doing everything he could to make life easier for her. Then, one day, a messenger boy arrived and called Adam out into the yard to deliver a message from Goldschmidt. "Sir, Mr. Goldschmidt wants you to come to Southampton to discuss a fight."

"Did he tell you who he wanted me to fight?"

"I think it is McMullens."

"Thank you. Go tell him that I will see him at noon at

his shop on the morrow."

Rebecca had a concerned look on her face when Adam returned to the cottage.

"What was that about, Adam?"

"Nothing to concern you, dear. Just a little business I have with Isaac."

"Horses, Adam? Is it about horses?"

Adam thought to himself that if he told Rebecca the truth that it might upset her. She could lose the baby in her delicate condition. So, he lied to her.

"Yes, it's about the deal to sell New Forest ponies to the miners."

"Wonderful, I was so nervous. I can't stand the thought of you ever again risking your life in the ring for money. I would rather eat old bread crusts than for you to do that again."

Adam felt ashamed to have to lie to the woman that he loved. But he couldn't jeopardize her health or the health of his unborn child by telling her the truth. Besides, Adam felt that this one fight would get him to a point financially where he could comfortably support his people while they spent time gathering ponies and breaking them so that they could be sold in the upcoming mining venture with Isaac.

At noon the following day Adam entered Isaac's shop. "Isaac, do you have some good news for me?"

"Yes I do, my associates were at a sportsman meeting in London and the promoter for the Irishman McMullen asked them to contact me about setting up a match with you."

"I've seen the man fight and he is very good, but so were a lot of other men I have come up against."

"Well, there were a lot of swells there who want this

fight to happen. They got together a purse. Win or lose, each of you will take away 150 pounds and the winner an extra 200 pounds. But the kicker was that Judge Kingsley was there and he was seriously inquiring about what the odds might be on you."

"Isaac, I know that I should be thankful, for I have been blessed with my wife and my freedom. I wouldn't consider ever fighting again, but I swore on a Bible in prison that before I died, I would punish the man for what he did to my brother Charles and my dear Vashti and my two boys - leaving them without a mother. I will take this match and I want to know everything Kingsley does in the way of betting."

A week later, Adam entered Isaac's shop and what he heard put a smile on his face. "Adam, your man seems to have a lot of confidence in you. He's wagered 2000 pounds on your winning."

The match with McMullen took place outside of London on a drizzly, overcast day. The field around the ring was muddy and crowded with men from every walk and stratum of life. Isaac called Adam's attention to an enclosed Hansom cab, which was parked behind the crowd two hundred feet away. "That's your man, Kingsley. Come to see you fight, but he doesn't want anyone to see him here."

"Good, I'll put on a good show for him. I'll let him get his money's worth."

Adam put on a good show and for most of the fight, he gave as good as he got. In the fifteenth round, after receiving a solid blow to his face, he went down and stayed down for the count. When Adam finally got up, he could see that Judge Kingsley was furious. He was yelling out of his cab window and shaking his fist towards the ring. "I'm not done with you yet Gypsy! You've had your day! You and your Jew accomplices! You'll come across my docket again, one of these times and you will pay for this!"

Adam took his revenge and his 200 pounds and he went home a tired and sore, but satisfied, man. Rebecca was very upset when she saw his condition. "Adam, why did you lie to me and do this to yourself?"

"I'm sorry, Rebecca. I would never have fought again for your sake. But I heard that your father was betting a lot of money on me, so I took the fight to lose and punish him. I swore a sacred oath that I would."

Rebecca forgave Adam for lying to her. She noticed now, once that he had punished her father, he seemed a much happier person. Soon Adam and Rebecca's child was born. It was a girl and Rebecca allowed Adam to name her Mirelli in honor of his grandmother who had helped raise him. As soon as Mirelli could walk, Rebecca took her along with her to work. Mirelli was no trouble, she fit in with the other children at the mission school and the other children begged to watch her.

# Chapter 17

L ife was sweet until one day eighteen year old Levi was traveling in the vicinity of Winchester. He came upon a constable who was viciously driving a sick old Gypsy man from his camp beside a country lane.

"I will see to it that you scum cease to pollute the verges of our local lanes. If you don't have this tent and all of your rubbish off of this roadside in an hours time, I'll fine you and impound what little you have got. So, old man, be quick about it. I'm already late for me supper."

The old man didn't say a word. He just tried to oblige the overbearing constable. He hitched his horse to his cart then he began to dismantle his tent, loading the pieces into his wagon. It was evident that he was not well and very short of breath. Levi approached, "Uncle, sit down and let me load your wagon." Levi had the old man sit on a wooden storage box. "You sit here and catch your breath."

The constable became furious. He grabbed the frail old man by the collar of his coat and lifted him from his resting place. "You sorry excuse of a man, you will not rest on my watch."

"Take your hands off of him!" Levi ordered the officer.

"And what business it our yours?"

"There's no need to treat him so. Can you not see that he is old and sick?"

When the constable released his grip, the old man fell backwards, striking his head on the storage box. Blood began to drip from a gash on the side of his head. Levi leaned over to help the old man to his feet. In an instant, the constable took his staff and gave Levi a crack across his back which caused him to fall beside the old man.

"You're down now. Stay down or I will bust your head wide open."

Levi looked up at the grinning constable who was straddling him. The slovenly dressed officer had neglected to properly button his crotch flap. Levi instinctively reached up through the opening in the man's trousers and grabbed a handful of the constables bulging privates. Levi squeezed and twisted the package until the rogue lawman was on his knees begging him for mercy. When he tried to strike out at Levi, Levi squeezed his gonads harder and he nearly fainted from the pain.

"I am going to let go of your figs, and when I do, I want you to leave this man be. He will move on with my help. If I see you again, I will rip these off and make you eat them. Are we agreed?"

The constable gave Levi a hateful look and hesitated. Levi gave the package a final hard squeeze.

"Yes! Yes! Please! Please!"

Levis released the constable. The constable straightened up and took a deep breath. He then picked up his staff and walked over to the old man. "You caused all of this trouble. It will be straight to the workhouse with you if ever I see you on my lanes again."

"Constable, you really are a glutton for punishment. Why have you not learned your lesson?"

"What lesson, Gypsy?"

"That a smart man can change his mind but a damn fool never will?"

"I'll show you who's a damn fool."

The constable swung his staff at Levi. Levi caught the staff with both hands and wrenched it from him. In short order, Levi raised the staff up and came back down with it hard upon the constable's head. The staff cracked in half and the constable fell to the ground like a dead weight and lay there unconscious.

The old man looked at the constable, then at Levi. "I hope you didn't *moor*(kill) him *chavy*(child), even though no one would deserve it more. He's a real *bengler*(devil) and he's *chored*(stolen) from us and molested our young *racklys(girls)* he found alone on the road."

"If he's dead, I say good riddance to him, uncle. Let's have a look at that cut on your head, then get you packed up. We shouldn't be around when or if he wakes."

"You're Adam Stanley's boy aren't you?"

Levi nods. "Levi is my name, uncle, *so's tuttie's nav*(what is your name)?"

"I'm Handsome Sampson Cooper. I was coming from Redding on my way to visit my sister in Christchurch when I got sick a few days ago. I decided to rest here for a spell. The *muscar*(constable) come by and warned me once to leave, but I was too knackered. That's why he was such a *koori*(prick) to me when he came back today and found me still here."

Levi and Sampson Cooper didn't realize it, but the constable had been playing dead. He was listening all the while they were loading the wagon, hearing the names of his assailants and where he could find them.

Levi finished loading Sampson's wagon and they were soon on their way. When the sound of their departing died down in the ears of the constable, he stood and felt his wounded head. He picked up the pieces of his broken staff to then meandered his way home to his late supper.

When Levi and Sampson got to Southampton, they parted ways, and Levi made his way back home to Fareham.

Adam was just coming out of the woods with his coursing dog and a clutch of fresh killed rabbits when Levi arrived tired and dirty from his battle with the Constable. "What happened to you, son? You look like you have been through the war."

"I have been through a battle, with a *muscar(constable)*. He was driving old Sampson Cooper from the side of the road. The *chur purri moush*(poor old man)was *naflo*(sick). *He* couldn't hardly stand up and the *suving muscar*(frigging constable) was choking him and pushing him around."

"*So'd ya ker*(what'd you do) to him?"

"He *delled*(hit) me across my back with a *bora cosh*(big stick). I took it away from him and cracked his scull with it."

"You didn't kill him, did you, son?"

"I hit him hard. But he was still breathing when I left him."

"Did he know you?"

"He just knows that I'm a Romnichel."

"You have to lay low for a few days until I can find out if the man is dead, or if the *gav foki gin*(town officials know) who you are."

"Okay, Dad, but before I *gaver my kucker adre* the

*vesh*(hide myself in the forest), could you get Tom to clean those *shoshoi*(rabbits) and mother to cook them? I haven't ate a bite in *dui divvus'*(two days)."

Adam laughed and hugged Levi. Levi winced a bit from his sore back. Adam lifted Levi's shirt to see a black bruise and welt running straight across his back.

"He got you good, son. Next time keep your eyes on your enemy."

"I got no excuses, Dad. I learned my lesson. If there is a next time."

Adam saddled his horse and rode straight to Southampton. He made his way to Isaac's shop. Isaac was surprised to see him. "What brings you to town, friend?"

"I need you to find any news you can about a constable who was assaulted while shifting some Gypsies from the roadside near Winchester yesterday."

"Your family?"

"My son Levi did the deed while defending an old man."

"When I find the information, Adam, I will send a messenger to you."

"Thanks, and how are preparations coming along for the shipment of the horses to your homeland?"

"Quite well. We can start boarding stock in Portsmouth next week. I sure wish you would come along. It's going to be quite an adventure."

"No, Isaac. I like to stay close to home. I've had enough adventure to last me two lifetimes."

"Well then, if you change your mind, there will be a place for you."

"Save that spot. You may have a passenger from my family but it won't be me."

"Then I will do my best to find out what happened in

Winchester."

A messenger arrived at Adam's cottage the following day. He handed Adam a sealed envelope. Adam took it into his cottage and placed it in Rebecca's hands. Rebecca opened the envelope and pulled from it a newspaper clipping from Winchester. To Adam's relief, she read that the constable was not killed. Rather, he identified his assailant as a Gypsy named Stanley with Levi's description. Isaac also included a note suggesting that Levi be brought to his apartment at night. There he could hide until the shipment of ponies to Romania was ready. Then, Levi could escape the country until the trouble died down.

At dusk, Adam sent Tom out into the forest with two horses. Tom went to an old abandoned charcoal burners camp where Levi was hiding. Tom gave Levi the news about the constable and told him to ride to Isaac's shop and hide there. Levi rode through the night until he reached Isaac's shop. When he reached the shop, he could see that the lights were burning bright in the Goldschmidt's living quarters above the shop. Levi rang the bell and Isaac answered the door. "Levi, glad to see you took your father's advice and came to me."

"Thank you, Mr. Goldschmidt. I'm tired. Do you have a place in your shop where I can sleep?"

"Sure I do, but first come up to my apartment. Sarah and I are having a late dinner."

Levi was taken upstairs where he was greeted by Sarah and her three lovely daughters. "Levi, this is my wife Sarah, and my daughters - Nadia, Naomi, and Julia."

Levi smiled and nodded his head as each of the females addressed him. "Pleased to meet you ladies, but I wish it was under different circumstances."

Sarah answered, "We are just having dinner. We would

be honored if you would join us."

"Thank you, I certainly will."

The table was laden with Jewish delicacies. Levi sat at the end of the table in a position of honor. The girls all tried to talk to Levi at the same time until Sarah took control and bade them, "Be quiet and let the young man eat his dinner."

Levi was wined and dined, then he was brought to a comfortable pallet that Sarah had prepared for him on the corner of her living room floor. Levi laid down and tried to sleep but the strangeness of his surroundings and the sound of tinkling dishes being put away and the giggling of Isaacs twittered daughters kept him up until midnight.

A local constable came to Adam's cottage the very next day. He was accompanied by another strange-looking constable who had a large knot in the center of his forehead. "Stanley where is your son?"

"Which son?"

"The older one. Constable Wiggins here was assaulted by a young Gypsy man near Winchester four day ago."

"What has this to do with my son?"

"The assailant seems to fit your son's description and he was a Stanley."

"Well, why don't you take your wounded man here to Derbyshire to Lord Stanley's estate and let him look for his assailant there? Lord Stanley has sons that look like my son."

"Where is your son?"

"My son is travelling. I have no idea where he is at this moment."

"Traveling, eh, that sounds suspicious to me."

"Suspicious? A Gypsy traveling is no more suspicious than settled person staying in the same place."

"When he returns, you see to it that he comes to me and we will see what he has to say for himself."

Adam nods and closes his door. The injured constable stood silent all the while during the exchange. When they left and started to walk down the lane he threw up his arms and started yelling at the local constable. "What kind of lawman are you? You let the Gypsies run you. I would have grabbed that Gypsy by his scruff and rolled around on ground with him until he told me where his son was."

"Is that so? Mr. Wiggins, I've a mind to let you put your money where your mouth is. Come on back with me and you show me how you can grab Gypsy Adam, the champion bare knuckle boxer of South England, and roll around on the ground with him."

The constable stood for a moment staring at Wiggins, in order to gauge his reaction. Wiggins spun on his heels and raced away towards town. "Come on, come on. I got to get to the inn before I'm late for me supper."

The following days that Levi spent at Isaac's were idyllic. He loved Sarah's food and sweet desserts. He enjoyed playing cards with and talking to Isaac's daughters. He would spend his days in Isaac's basement jewelry shop where Isaac showed him some of the tricks of the jewelry trade and how to cast gold bracelets and rings.

Adam tried to bribe the constable into dropping charges against Levi but to no avail. Rebecca wrote a letter to her father asking for his help in the matter, but he refused to even send her a reply. Adam concluded that the safest thing for Levi to do was to leave the country.

Adam sent Isaac a package of clothing to give to Levi for his trip. He placed his own sturdy velveteen jacket inside the package. It was specially tailored with a row of hidden plankets for the gold sovereign buttons. The jacket could remain open in warmer weather without the sovereigns showing. Adam knew that if Levi got himself into trouble in a foreign land, he could use the sovereigns to buy his way out.

Adam steered clear of Portsmouth for the next week, so as not to draw attention to the ship or Levi. He let Isaac handle the business of recording the consignments of ponies from the various Romnichel families involved in the venture so that the profits could be equitably shared when Isaac returned from Romania.

Now all Isaac had to do was turn an 18-year-old Gypsy fellow into Jewish woman so that he could get him safely to his ship and out of the country.

The Goldschmidt family woke early and Sarah prepared a nice breakfast of coddled eggs, toasted bread and marmalade. And now the work began. Sarah went through her whole wardrobe and finally found a dress that would fit Levi's frame. It was a sturdy gray dress made of cotton with a matching cape of cotton duck. The only female shoes she could find were and old pair of her dead mother's shoes that were from the basement. These shoes made Levi nervous. He wasn't highly superstitious, but most of the older Romanies believed that the spirits of the dead inhabited their possessions, including their clothing. That is why Gypsies burned the possessions of their dead, so that these objects would not prevent spirits from passing into the otherworld. Levi told Isaac about this belief and he answered. "Mozel tov, let us hope that the spirit of Babushka dwells within you boy. We are going to need all of the help that we can get to pull this off."

The Goldschmidt girls surrounded Levi. They were having a good time trying to feminize his darkly handsome features. Naomi searched and came up from the shop with a kit of stage makeup which had been pawned by a traveling actor. "Look what I have found. Now we can make Levi look like Jezebel." Sarah took over, putting just the right touches of rouge and lip color on Levi to make him a convincing Jewess at least enough to get him through town and onto the ship without suspicion.

The moment of truth had come. Isaac loaded his wife and daughters into his carriage. He seated Levi in the back seat between his pretty daughters. They made the trip without incident. Isaac and Levi said their goodbyes to Isaac's family, while Sarah took the reins. Isaac escorted the tall awkward character up the gang plank onto the ship. Several of the old sailors that Isaac had hired for the trip perked up when they saw Levi. "Hello, Miss, welcome aboard."

Levi held his hand to partially cover his face. He hurried past the old sailors and quickly made his way to his appointed cabin.

Romania

# **Chapter 18**

The main sails filled and the ropes creaked against the ship's tackle blocks. Levi stood on the forecastle and watched with relief as the shoreline of the Isle of Wight shrank away in the distance.

At this moment, he was experiencing two very conflicting feelings. One was the relief that he was escaping the spectre of serving unjust prison time for protecting an old man from the brutality of a cruel enforcers of his country's unfair highway laws. The other strange feeling was that of having been dressed as a female for nearly a whole day and it was driving him mad. "Isaac, I must rip these clothes off! I cannot bear another moment having these toothless old swabbies ogling me as if I were a piece of Christmas cake."

"Now just you hold your bloomers on, Levi. You must keep the sailors happy for just a few more days until we pass through Gibralter. There we could be boarded by the Royal Navy and have our manifest and passenger list checked. We would have to do a lot explaining if we couldn't present the beautiful Miss Rosenbaum from the passenger list."

After passing Gibralter and heading into the Mediterranean Sea, Isaac finally relented and told Levi that he could shed his female persona. Levi went into his cabin and changed into male garb. He put the female clothing in a bag and carried it to the side of the ship where he threw it into the water. One of the old sailors discovered him and observed him disposing of something. He sounded the alarm. "Stow away! Captain!, stow away!" Levi laughed when the old sailor said, "Who are you? What did you throw overboard?"

"Oh, that was the last of Miss Rosenbaum. I ravaged her, and then I killed her. I cut her up into little pieces and I threw her into the water."

The old sailor was horrified. He turned to find Isaac laughing. "Did you hear what this man did?"

"Yes, and what he threw in the water was Miss Rosenbaum's clothing. She is still alive, but she's turned herself into this man."

Levi and Isaac laughed as the old sailor shook his head and walked away feeling very sheepish.

The rest of the trip was uneventful. Upon arriving in Romania, Levi was horrified to find that the Gypsies there had been living in the state of slavery for centuries. They were the possessions of the state, the church, and the *Boyars*(landed gentry).

Levi witnessed many scenes of cruelty towards the Gypsies and though they differed from him in appearance and language dialect, he still saw them as his people. All this brutality and oppression was causing hatred for the non-Gypsies around him to well up inside him, like a bitter bile in his throat that would not go away.

There was another type of Gypsy in Romania, the Netotsi. These were forest people who lived freely in inaccessible areas of the mountains. They were ferocious guerrilla fighters and were feared by all Romanians, even the militias. The Netotsi were tall and very dark with jet black hair and brilliant white teeth. On the rare occasion that one of the grown Netotsi was captured, they very seldom made good slaves. They often died in their confinement or were beaten to death by their overseers.

As Isaac and Levi's party were driving their herd of horses through the mountains to the mining town, they passed a group on *Zlatari*(gold-washing Gypsies). They were naked, except for a black grease smeared over their bodies to protect them from the ice cold water. They stood waist-deep in the water while they shoveled gravel and sand into a gold sluice. Each man had a hideous triangular, wooden collar with metal spikes in it around his neck. These were called "cangues." All of the gold that they sifted went to their master who stood over them with a whip. Several of the Zlatari squatted by a fire and drew from it blacked pieces of corn meal mush,*mamaliga* which was their basic food.

That evening, the party arrived at the estate of Theodor Ciobanu - a wealthy Boyar who was an old acquaintance of Isaac's. He greeted them with much hospitality. After they settled into their primitive but comfortable accommodations, they were treated to a sumptuous meal by the Mr. Ciobanu who fancied himself quite an enlightened individual. This was in spite of the fact that he was in possession of more than 100 Gypsy slaves. Even among these slaves there were castes. The agricultural and worker slaves were poorly dressed and taken care of by their masters. They slept in barns, sheds, and cellars. The house slaves were better dressed and acted in a more refined manner as they were always in close contact with the master's family.

While Levi and Isaac were dining with their host and two other guests, two middle-aged French men who were also in Romania on business matters, a beautiful Gypsy girl who was serving them caught Levi's eye. Her name was Stella. She was of fair complexion and had brilliant green eyes. Mr. Ciobanu noticed Levi's fascination with Stella, "Young gentleman, would you like to bed her tonight?"

"Bed her, Sir? What do you mean?"

"I am offering you a night of pleasure with her. Do you accept?"

This upset Levi. He was angered that this *gauja* had such god-like control over one of his own. He hesitated momentarily and then noticing the lecherous stares that the Frenchmen were giving Stella, he answered, "Yes, thank you. I very much would like the pleasure of her company."

After the meal, several strong drinks and long discussions, between the Boyar, Isaac and the Frenchmen. Levi excused himself and retired to his candle-lit room. Shortly thereafter, Stella arrived. Levi was not aggressive with her, she was surprised by his kindness and gentleness. Levi spoke to her in Romany, placing his hand on his chest, "Romnichel." Stella didn't understand the term. Levi tried again, "*Tsigan*(Gypsy), me *Tsigano* English." Stella cried and hugged him. Levis sat with Stella and they become acquainted by means of a strange mixture of whatever Gypsy words they had in common, as well as sign language. Eventually the language of love took over and

Levi snuffed out the candle.

When Levi awakened in the morning, he found that Stella had risen before him and was already at her chores. Levi dressed, did his morning ablutions and found Isaac who was getting his men ready for the journey to the market town. "How was your night, Levi?"

Levi was perplexed. He couldn't find the right words to use to explain the thoughts that were flying through his brain and the anxious feeling that filled his stomach. "Isaac, I love her."

"You love her? What is this you are telling me? She is a slave and the property of the Boyar."

"I can't leave her. I have never been with a woman like that. I don't know what to do."

"Well, I can't leave you here with her. You would have to take on her status as a slave."

"Well, will you talk to the Boyar and see if he will sell her?"

"Levi, I will do my best but you must realise that she may be worth all that we possess."

"Isaac you must try at least - please, for me. Do your best."

Isaac walked into the Mr.Ciobanu's house and, thirty minutes later, he came out with a smile on his face and Stella on his arm. "How did you do it?"

Isaac released Stella to Levi's loving embrace. He didn't answer Levi, but turned and ordered his drovers to remove his fancy saddle from his beautiful white Arabian stallion.

"What are you doing, Isaac?"

"Mr. Ciobanu would take nothing less for your Stella. He figured he could make more money and at a faster rate by siring foals from my Arabian stallion than he could by breeding slaves from your Stella. Besides, he said he had a soft spot for you. He didn't want you to leave his house a disappointed man."

Levi knew that he would have to repay Isaac for his horse and his expenses from his tribe's money. There would be repercussions when he arrived home, but he had never been happier.

As Isaac's party entered the town where the stock auction was taking place Levi saw a poster advertising Gypsy slaves for sale. Isaac, too, saw the poster. They both got down from their horses and Isaac read aloud the notice: "For sale, a fine lot of Gypsy slaves. Consisting of eight men, four women, six boys and three girls all in good condition. May eighth at the Brasov Cattle Auction." Levi became angry and tore the broadside to pieces.

Just as Isaac expected when they arrived at the bustling market town, it was crowded with wealthy Boyars and mine owners.

After all of their horses had been sold and the money collected, Levi and Isaac watched as a wagon load of pitiful Gypsy slaves arrived. They were roughly ushered up to the auction block for inspection and sale. Levi watched as boisterous and cheerful Boyars and their peasant overseers examined the Gypsies. Some of the men even opened the ragged blouse of a teenage girl so that they might feel and comment on her breasts. Levi vowed to himself that he would buy this family of Gypsies, no matter if it took all of his people's money.

Levi had Isaac do the bidding and as the group was being sold piecemeal, crying children were separated from their parents and older brothers and sisters. The anguish of each of the family members diminished with each successful bid, and they saw that they would not be separated.

Levi's had to spend his people's share of the horse profits to buy the Gypsy slave family. He was now broke and wondering how he was going to pay Isaac back for the horse that was traded for Stella when a commotion broke out, just as they were getting ready to leave. A slave handler with a long mustache struggled with a wild looking young Netotsi man. The Netotsi was chained with an iron collar around his neck and he was struggling for all that he was worth. Another handler slashed his back with a bullwhip and drew blood. The Netotsi cursed his handlers and spit at them. As he turned and was brought to the auction block, Levi saw that his back was corded with the scars of countless other whippings. Levi was broke but he struggled with his conscience as each bid drew the sale of this brother Gypsy's life closer to a torturous end.

In an act of desperation and total loss of control, Levi exploded and poured out a stream of curses in Romany. He began to rip his jacket off, causing several gold coin buttons to break loose and spill onto the floor in front of the auctioneer. The auctioneer walked over and picked up the gold sovereigns and examined them. He held four fingers up to Levi, smiled and said in Romanian, *inca patru va rog* (four more please). Levi understood and forcefully ripped the rest of his jacket open freeing the remaining gold coin buttons. The Autioneer held up the gold coins and asked for a higher bid, none came. No one could top Levi's bid, so he was handed the chain hooked to the Netotsi's neck. Levi threw the end of the chain at the slave handler's legs and motioned for him to remove the lock from the Netotsi's collar. The nervous handler handed Levi the key and quickly retreated. Levi unlocked and removed the collar, bundled the chain and threw it at the handler.

The Netotsi was surprised at what had just happened.

131

He looked for a moment into Levi's eyes, then he smiled and reached out and shook his hand and said in Romany, "Paraka tu mirro phral"(thank you, my brother). "Let us go from among these swine." Then the whole party began its trek to the flatboat which was waiting to float them down the river to the port where Isaac's ship was anchored.

The Netotsi's name was Laishy. He had been captured five years earlier and he had been a gold-washer for a cruel master who finally got tired of his wild spirit and sold him. Isaac, speaking in his native Romanian told Laishy all about England. Laishy was very excited about accompanying him to this strange new land where Gypsies roamed free.

Often Gypsy gold washers would steal gold nuggets by furtively swallowing them. They would recover them later and hide their stashes in the forest to use in the event they could escape or become connected with certain people who might be able to use the gold to buy their freedom. Laishy was no exception. He had several gold stashes hidden in the rocks along the river. At times, he would dive off of the boat and swim ashore, disappear into the forest for several minutes, then reappear on the bank ahead of the boat. He would stand there with a sly smile on his face, then he would swim back out to the boat with his little leather pouches of gold nuggets held firmly in his teeth. Each time he found one of his stashes he gave the gold to Levi and thanked him for what he had done for him. As Laishy passed other Gypsy Zlatari on the river, he would cry out in Romany to them and tell them of his good luck. They shouted back to him, "Latcho! latcho!(good,good)". By the time they reached the port, Levi had all of his profits back and then some. He borrowed some cash from

Isaac, then he and Stella went shopping for decent clothes for her, Laishy, and the Gypsy family. When Levi saw the way that Stella handled the merchants he knew that when he got her back to England and turned her loose on the public he had a Gypsy wife who would make him proud.

Levi got to know all of the Romanians on the voyage home. The father of the group was a blacksmith by the name of August Stankovitch. His wife was a talented basket weaver named Annya. The two teenaged sons were accomplished coppersmiths, and the two younger children were adorable and well-behaved until they found out that they could get away with anything. Then, they were the terror of the crew.

Before Isaac left England, he had instructed his wife Sarah to monitor the situation concerning Levi and the constable. He requested, too, that she send weekly letters to his cousin in Gibralter. If things were still too hot in England, then Levi could stay in Gibralter until it was safe for him to return home.

Sarah's latest letter had just arrived when Isaac anchored in Gibralter and visited his cousin. It contained some very good news for Levi. It seems that constable Wiggins had been arrested for molesting two aristocratic teenage girls who, for a lark, had dressed as Gypsies and were walking on country lanes.

England
# Chapter 19

When Levi arrived home, he and his Romanian friends trekked into New Forest where his family and the rest of the tribe awaited the profits of the horse sale. The Romnichels became upset when they saw Levi coming down the road with a large group of foreign Gypsies. They accused Levi of being crazy, "Haven't we got enough people to feed around here? Why would you bring these foreign Gypsies on us?" Levi became angry. He removed Laishy's shirt and showed them his scarred back. "This boy was being beat to death when I bought him at a horse auction. These children were being sold away from their mother and father, just like we hear about the Negro slaves in America. I know that they're a different sort of Gypsy from us, but they deserve some kind of life. They were living in a land where they were treated worse than you would treat an animal."

Levi's relatives were ashamed and saddened. They couldn't believe what they had heard. They took Gus and his family and Laishy and welcomed them to their camp. They fed them and gave them blankets, pots and pans and helped them make a little shelter in which to sleep. When morning arrived, the Romnichels arose and went about their business of making clothes pegs and baskets. Annya watched how the Romnichel women wove their basket, then she took up some willow branches. In a short time, she executed a beautiful basket design that put the English Gypsy baskets to shame.

One of the Romnichel women examined Aanya's basket, and exclaimed, "*dordi, dick duver!*(Lord, look at that!)" In no time at all, Annya had the whole camp taking basket weaving lessons.

Gus took his two sons to town and he purchased some tools and solder. They went about town and communicating in their broken English they managed to collect more damaged copper pots and pans than they could comfortably carry back to the camp for repairs. The men of the camp were very pleased when they saw that the Romanian's commercial activities would not compete with theirs.

# Chapter 20

The Stanley family seemed to have finally found peace and harmony and years have passed without incident. Adam and Rebecca's daughter, Mirelli, has grown into a pretty, coquettish sixteen year old. She had her father's hazel eyes, her mother's rosey cheeks and light brown hair.

Tom and Levi saw to it that their little sister was well-versed in Romnichel lore and language. They would fight any Romnichel boy at the mission who dared to call her a "*posh rat*(half-blood)."

Her big brothers would while away their hours telling Merelli stories and riddles. This to not only entertain her but to sharpen her wit. One day, Tom tried to stump Merelli. "Water over, water under, and I am as dry as a bone. What am I?"

Mirelli smiled and quickly retorted, "You, Tom, would be - ah - a maid carrying a pitcher of water on your head while you walked across a bridge."

"How did you know that? Me and Uncle Wester were the only ones that knew that riddle."

"Silly *chor(boy)*, Aunt Richanda told me. Ha! Ha! A

136

fine maid you would make with those beautiful eyes of yorn, a lovely, lovely maid." Mirelli couldn't stop laughing as she and Levi absorbed a few soft shoulder taps from their embarassed brother.

Rebecca saw to it that Mirelli could read well, cook, sew and always carry herself in a ladylike manner. But Mirelli idolized Aunt Richanda and chose her as a role model, preferring her style of cooking, philosophy and way of talking and carrying herself.

Now that Mirelli was a young woman, Aunt Richanda thought that it was time to teach her the ultimate Romnichel female occupation. A vocation that she could carry with her wherever she went. A vocation that could never be taken away from her and one that she could always depend on to support herself and her family. A trade that had been passed down from mother to daughter for a thousand years. A way to earn a profit without the expenditure of a moments physical labor or a farthing for stock, fortune telling.

"Merelli, I've taught you to peddle with the best of them. You can *rokker*(speak) to anyone and you have the gift to charm the old *beng*(devil). I want to take you out and teach you to be a proper *dukkering juvel(fortune teller)*."

"Aunt, no disrespect to you, but I can't. I got certain principles and I couldn't do it - even if it were just to entertain the women at a *gauja* church party."

"Now child, I've never stole money nor misled a soul to do anything that would harm them. God gave us Romnichels the gift of *dukkering* to feed us in a world where every man was against us and would kill us and would begrudge us a crust of bread. As we traveled through a hostile world, *dukkering* was the only thing that they could not take from us. It is the gift that keeps giving. It can be used for both good or bad."

"Aunt, I know that you *dukkered* to put bread on your table. But I couldn't feel good about deceiving those silly women, putting dreamy thoughts about imaginary lovers in their heads and taking their money. It just ain't me, aunt. But I thank you for offering to teach me. My mother showed me in the Bible where it was ungodly to *dukker*. Please don't get angry with me. I just don't want to get up to it."

"Alright Merelli, I respect you have a mind to do as you wish. But I want you to know that sometimes I use *dukkering* to help people by telling them the right thing to do. Some poor souls don't have no one to talk to and confide in. The guilt and secrets that they hold are just too much for them. It can cause them to do bad things to themselves and others. So, you see, I do earn my money when I help them out with sensible advice. I never get any pleasure from cheating or making fools of the dear people no matter how silly or ignorant they is."

"I know, aunt. I know you are a good, God-fearing woman. I seen how you put money in poor and hungry *foki's* hands. But please, I just don't feel that I have the gift for *dukkering*. Maybe it's the *gauja* in me."

"Child, don't say that. Your blood and your dear mother's blood is like my own. You are no different than my own child. If I had a daughter, then I would want her to be just like you."

"Thank you, aunt."

"Well, Merelli, if you can't dukker then you must peddle. There are things that a young woman like yourself must know about taking care of your reputation around men and boys, especially when you're out alone *opre* the *drum*(upon the road) a *bikoning*(selling)."

Mirelli respected her great-aunt and valued her advice, but she was getting uncomfortable as Aunt Richanda began talking more and more to her about the opposite sex. The climax of this phase of Gypsy sex education came one day when Aunt Richanda approached Merelli holding a small ancient wooden box. She opened it to reveal a small leather thong with long leather strings attached. "When I was a young girl, my mother brought this *diklo* made of rabbit hide to me and told me to put it on. She said, 'Here *chi*(daughter). I wore this as a girl and it protected me, now it is your turn to wear it."

Aunt Richanda held up the heirloom Gypsy chastity belt and showed Merelli that it was still supple and very functional.

"You see, child, me mother would tie this on me every time I would go out alone a peddling on the road. She knew that I was a flirtatious girl and that I acted like a devil every time I got around good-looking young men. So she tied this *diklo* up on me with a special knot in the back that only she knew. If it ever were untied she would know that the seal was broken."

"Aunt what would you do if nature called?"

"See child, the little hole in the front? that would work fine if you had to go *muter*(pee)."

"Oh aunt, it must have been very unpleasant to wear."

"T'was at first, but I was a wild girl and the fellas would follow me around, trying to get me to *jal adre* the *vesh*(go into the woods)with them. I kissed a few, but my *diklo* and the fear of my mother kept me pure for your Uncle Wester. You see, if a Romany girl is not a virgin, our men won't want them."

"Well that's no surprise. Decent gauja moushes don't want no trollop either."

"Merelli, child, you got a good head on your shoulders but one day your thoughts will be on *rummering*(marriage), just like mine was when I first saw your Uncle Wester. I was about your age and I noticed how strong and handsome he was, but he was real shy around me. No matter how hard I tried, I couldn't get him to pay me no attention. He acted like he was always busy having to do something or other for his daddus. Even when I came around and tried to flirt with him. He was a hard nut to crack. He was real *atrashed*(afraid) of his daddus and, when his old father saw me coming, he would give me a *vasavo dick*(bad look). He then put Wester to work. He would say, 'Man's face get over here and take care of the *grys*.' He would slap Wester sometimes - not hard, but just enough to get his attention. Then, he would say you ain't man enough to take care of your *kucker*(self). How could you *lel a juvel*(get a woman)? Poor old Uncle Wester, his father really gave him a hard time."

"If things was that bad, aunt, how ever did you get him away from his father?"

"Well, child, I used a special old Romnichel trick. One day, I seen him out all alone by the river a watering his daddus' horses. I snuck up behind him with a bita lady smell on my fingers."

"Lady smell, aunt, what's that?"

"*Minge*(vagina), my dear."

"Oh."

"Now I went up to Wester and asked him if he could figure out what this strange smell that I had got on my fingers was. He fell for it, and as I placed my fingers under his nose, he took a deep wiff. Then, I couldn't help but laugh. He realized right away what I had done, and he called me a '*Bitta lubni*(little whore).' But my trick worked, you know. After that, he snuk away every chance he could to be with me, even though he knew his father would thrash him for it. They say that when a young *moush* gets a wiff of *minge* then there ain't much a father can do with him. We runned away together the very next month and *lelled rummered*(got married). When we came back to our people, they was real loving and civil with us, they all gave us presents. His old dad even hugged me and called me daughter."

"That was quite a story, aunt. And thanks for telling me about that trick. Though I don't think that I could ever be as brash as you to use it."

"Well, at least now you know that us women possess a special power over men and it's *tatchi*(true)."

"That was funny and crafty, but I'm not concerned with *moushes* yet. Aunt, there will be plenty of time for that later on. Besides, my mother and father don't approve of me going out peddling alone on the road. So, aunt, put that thing away and please don't show it to mother. She might take it wrong and get offended."

Early one morning Mirelli was left alone to tend the cottage. Against her parents orders, she decided to try to earn a little money and surprise them. She put on her *munging*(begging) apron(used to carry food and keep it from being defiled by coming into contact with her dress). She filled a basket with hand-carved clothes and pegs, then began her walk to a neighboring village to peddle her wares or barter them for food.

In a manor house several miles away, Janet (a scullery maid) was at work polishing her employer's prize heirloom silverware. There was a knock at the door. She stopped her work, went to the door, and opened it to see a tall, strapping young red-headed man. "Oh, hello Bub. I didn't realise we had a meat delivery today."

"The squire must planning some parties soon or his appetite is growing. This is his biggest order of hams and sausages yet."

"Cousin, you do have the best sausage."

"Oh my, you are a caution, Janet."

"Who you got sitting out there in the wagon?"

"I brought Jim to help me today. I been a bit down in the back."

"Not too down in the back, I hope. I been kinda lonely for you. A girl don't get too much excitement around here. And I was hoping for a little stimulation - if you know what I mean, cousin."

"Oh, I know what you mean."

"Well then, let's get this provisioner business over. Then, we'll give it a go."

Jim loaded a small barrow with cured hams and assorted meats, then he wheeled it to the kitchen door. Bub and Jim took arm loads of meat to the pantry for Janet to put away. When Janet finished her job, she sat Jim at a small table in the corner of the kitchen and she poured him a cup of tea and gave him a small dish of pastries.

Janet looked sneakily around the house. Seeing that she was alone, she turned to the Bub, squeezed his arm, and gave him an, "Okay Bub, let's give it a go." Janet escorted Bub into the pantry and closed the door. As Jim kept watch, Bub and Janet carried on noisily behind the pantry door. Jim was oblivious to the distraction, for his eyes had caught the gleam of the ornate sterling silver spoon he was using to stir sugar into his tea. Jim looked across the room to see that the rest of the silverware was lying on a counter. While Bub was occupying Janet, Jim stole every piece of the silverware and secreted it in their cart. However, he missed one spoon which Janet had left wrapped in a polishing cloth.

Bub and Janet exited the pantry. Bub's face was flushed, and Janet was sweaty and disheveled. Janet gave Bub a sloppy kiss which was cut short by a shout from an anxious Jim who was waiting in the cart. "Come on, Romeo, we have meat to deliver!"

Another maid entered the kitchen. Her name was Venus, she and Janet were friends. Venus gave Janet one look and remarked, "Diddling with the sausage man again, heh? Ain't we living on the edge?" Janet answered Venus with a wink and a sigh, as her eyes hungrily followed the departure of her waving paramour.

Janet brushed back her hair and turned to Venus, "That man can make me liver quiver and me bladder splatter." Venus laughed at Janet's remark. Then, Janet returned to her job of putting away the silverware.

When Janet saw that the silver was gone, she lost her breath, "My God, it's gone!"

Venus grabbed the trembling Janet, "What?"

Janet answered, "Jim and Bub stole the silver."

"You must tell Squire Fenner."

Janet answered, "I can't tell on them. Jim and Bub are me cousins."

In the midst of confusion, the women heard someone whistling in the distance through the open doorway. It was Mirelli, whom was walking down the lane towards them with her basket in hand. Venus had a brainstorm. She quips, with cocksure confidence, "Look, see yonder Gypsy coming. I'll show you how to take care of this business - just you watch."

Venus took the last remaining piece of silverware and pushed it into the center of a loaf of bread. She then wrapped the bread in a dish cloth and handed it to Janet. "We'll put it off on the Gypsy. They're all about thievery anyway."

Janet breathed a sigh of relief. Both woman waited at the door of the kitchen for the poor unsuspecting Mirelli.

Mirelli greeted the women with a little huckster patter, "Good day to you, my ladies. Would you be interested in buying some clothes pegs?"

Janet opened the door wider. She reached into Mirelli's basket and drew out a bleached white wooden peg. She fingered and admired the shiny tin band around it. "They are well-made. How much a dozen?"

"I have a bargain for you nice ladies today. How about sixpence?"

Janet looked at Venus and gave her a wink. "Well then, miss, that sounds a fair price." Mirelli set her basket down and counted out a dozen clothes pegs. She handed them to Venus, and then she accepted payment from Janet. "Thank you, ma'am."

"Now Gypsy girl, how about telling us our fortunes?"

Mirelli blushed.

"I'm afraid that I'm not very good at that."

Janet pushed a silver coin into her hand, "Come now, Gypsy lassy. Don't be shy with us. All of you people are clairvoyant. I refuse to let you go unless you tell us our fortunes."

Mirelli tried to hand the coin back, "No please. I was raised a Christian, I can't."

"Oh yes can, and you will, or, you will give back to me what we gave you."

Janet mockingly taunted Merelli, "Come Gypsy, tell us what wondrous things await us in this world. Tell me, will I soon again have a lover and will he be a meatman?"

The trashy women laughed at their inside joke. To save face, Mirelli took each of the women's hands and supplied them with enough stock clairvoyant predictions to satisfy them.

Before she left, Mirelli asked the women for a *boon-tithe*. "Just a little gift of food so that you good ladies may be blessed."

Venus knew of this Gypsy custom and had waited for just this moment to give Merelli the loaf of bread containing the hidden spoon. Mirelli thanked them, placed the bread in her apron pouch and walked away. The cruel maids closed the door and laughed as they waited several minutes to sound the alarm on their innocent victim.

Mirelli was proud of herself. After she passed the gates of the estate, she stopped and patted the loaf of bread in her apron. She counted the coins in her hand and thought to herself, "Maybe I can be a fortune teller after all." Then, she continued on her way down the lane. Back at the estate, Janet stepped outside the rear door of the house and she began to yell, "Squire! The silver is gone, stolen by the Gypsy! She's gone down the lane! Stop her somebody, stop her!"

As Janet expected, Squire Fenner and one of his grooms ran from the stables behind the manor house. The maids led the way as they all bore down on the startled Mirelli. Squire Fenner grabbed Mirelli. "Filthy vagrant! Where are your accomplices! Where is my silver!"

As Mirelli proclaimed her innocence, Venus grabbed the loaf of bread from her apron and broke it in half in front of Fenner's face, exposing the silver spoon. Fenner flew into a fit of rage. He began to choke poor Mirelli. "Where is the rest of it? I'll see that you hang if you don't tell me where my silver is."

The more Mirelli proclaimed her innocence, the angrier Squire Fenner became.

Mirelli was taken up by a constable and brought before a judge before she could contact her family. The judge was her grandfather, Horatio Kingsley, but neither she nor the judge was aware of the fact. There were many cases being tried. Justice had to be swift just to clear the docket and make sure that the convict transports could be filled efficiently so that the proper commissions could be received by certain principals.

Judge Kingsley offered Mirelli a chance at leniency, "If you can tell me what you did with Squire Fenner's silver, then I will see that you receive a lighter sentence because of your youth. What do you say to that?"

Mirelli tearfully pleaded, "Sir, I know nothing of the silver. I was just peddling clothes pegs to the maidservants. I sold them some and that was all. I don't know why they would attack me and accuse me of this theft."

"I can see that you are a hard one, and you don't realise the seriousness of what you have done. So, I have no choice but to sentence you to be transported for seven years of hard service in Botany Bay. Luckey for you, young woman, you will be placed on a ship composed of women and children prisoners bound for Australia. I think that there is still time to get you aboard before they weigh anchor this evening." Mirelli was immediately sent to the waiting ship.

When Adam and Rebecca learned of Mirelli's arrest, they rushed to Kingsley's estate. Kingsley was shaken upon learning that Mirelli was his granddaughter and that the men who stole the silver had been caught when they tried to sell it to Isaac Goldschmidt, who had been alerted of the theft by Adam. Kingsley, Adam, and Rebecca rushed to the port but it was too late, her ship had already sailed. They tried frantically to find another ship but it was useless. High winds arose and it was several weeks before another ship set to sail for Australia.

Tom volunteered to go on the mission to bring his sister home. He was armed with a leather pouch full of gold sovereigns and Merelli's pardon and release papers, signed by Kingsley.

Aboard ship, Tom had a small cabin and he had brought along a trunk full of provisions to tide him over on his long voyage.

The captain of the ship's guard was an ogre named Lemmon. Lemmon was a sadistic pervert who relished tormenting his prisoners. When Tom saw how wretchedly the prisoners on his ship were treated, he worried for Mirelli's safety. Though Tom hated watching helplessly as Lemmon abused the transportees, Lemmon inadvertently offered Tom a little respite on the dull voyage - especially when Lemmon carried on and made over his big ugly gray cat which he affectionately referred to as his, "dear puss."

At night, Tom was distressed when he heard the screams of women prisoners down in the hold. He knew that Lemmon was molesting them, but all of his complaints to the drunken captain fell on deaf ears. "Mr. Stanley, my men have a job to do, just to keep this ship going and keep the prisoners in line. If you persist in interfering, then I will see to it that you get locked in the brig. Is that understood?"

"Understood, but I'll never understand how a man such as yourself ever got into such a position of authority."

"You can insult me all you want Stanley, but you had better tread lightly when it comes to my men."

Tom became acquainted with and befriended a fifteen

year old boy named Jimmy. The boy was transported with his mother and father who chose transportation rather than debtors prison. Lemmon always bullied the boy and ordered him about. One day, Lemmon had the boy taring chinks in a lifeboat for hours. he ordered the boy into the hold when night fell, where he attempted to abuse him. Tom heard them struggling and looked down through the wooden bars of the vent grate to see Lemmon pinning the boy down. Tom grabbed a bucket of tar that was nearby. He placed it on the grate above Lemmon's head. Tom snatched Puss who was milling around behind him. He pushed Puss's face down onto the grate, causing him to let out an angry growl. Lemmon stopped his attack on the boy and with concern he called up to his cat, "Puss, dear Puss, whatever is the matter?" In the dim light, Tom pushed Puss' head against the bucket causing tar to spill down and cover Lemmon from head to toe. Tom slipped away into the shadows with an overwhelming feeling of satisfaction. Lemmon came up out of the hold. He was crying and stumbling blindly about the deck. He cursed Puss and flailed at him. Puss climbed into the safety of the rigging. It took Lemmon several days to remove the tar. It was a nearly impossible task, he finally had to shave his head.

One of Lemmon's favorite pastimes was watching Tom eat his picnic meals on the deck, and Tom found joy in suffering Lemmon to watch him eat his canned meats, relishes, and marmalades. This subtle torture had driven Lemmon to the point that he was sneaking into Tom's vacant cabin and trying to break into his locked food trunk. Lemmon was getting deathly tired of his hard and wormy ships biscuits, his minuscule portions of rancid salt pork, and watery fish stews.

One day, Tom handed a partial can of beef to Jimmy who was sitting on the deck. Lemmon swooped down just as Jimmy began to enjoy this rare delicacy, ripping it from the boy's hands. He flew below deck to wolf it down. This angered Tom who had been watching from his cabin window.

Later that evening, Tom discovered Puss in his cabin with a half eaten rat. He yelled at Puss, causing him to drop the rat. Tom took a tin of meat from his trunk, opened it, and spooned out half of it onto some bread, this was dinner. Upon finishing his meal he took a knife and cut up the rat's carcass. He stirred the rat's flesh and guts into the half-empty can of meat and placed it in the rafters of his room.

Several days later, when Tom could no longer stand the smell of the rotten meat, he took the can down and proceeded with his plan to punish the gluttonous Mr. Lemmon. The next morning, Tom saw Jimmy airing himself on the deck. Jimmy was anxious to go along when Tom told him of his plan for the contaminated meat. Tom returned to his cabin, retrieving the can of meat and stirring it up with a spoon. Making sure that Lemmon was watching, Tom handed the can of contaminated meat to Jimmy. Then, he walked away. Jimmy put on a show and pretended to eat from the can. As Tom expected, Lemmon rushed up and wrested the can of meat from Jimmy. "That was mine. You're a thief, you are."

Lemmon smiled slyly at the boy as he put a large spoonful of rotten meat into his mouth. "Maybe I am, lad, but not a hungry one. Mmmm. This can is better than the last one I stole from ye, and kinda reminds me of me mother's stew."

Several hours later, Lemmon became violently ill. He

threw his head over the rail and vomited. He jerked his head up, erect, eyes popping. He reached for a wooden bucket, grabbed his gut, then he rushed below deck. It took Lemmon a long while to recuperate, but when he was again on his feet, he was back to his old game of badgering the inmates.

One evening, Lemmon got amorous as he watched Jimmy's mother wash her hair on deck. As she was drying her hair with a rag, he grabbed her and pressed his body against hers. He forced her below into a cell next to her husband and son, raping her. When he came topside, Tom was standing beside the rail, smoking a cigar. Tom was aware of what Lemmon had just done. He played it cool and offered Lemmon a smoke and a light from his glowing cigar. Tom placed a deceivingly friendly hand on Lemmon's shoulder and joked, "Hey Lemmon, my good man. Did you ever hear the one about the old gent who couldn't get enough?"

Lemmon was tickled by the attention, "No, Stanley, I don't think I have. Tell me it."

"Well," Tom says, "T'was the death of him."

Lemmon says, "I don't understand."

Tom, holding a wooden belaying pin behind his back, perked up. "Well, one night the old gent fell right in. At that moment, before Lemmon had time to react, Tom brought the club crashing down onto the back of Lemmon's skull. It sent him over the side of the ship into the dark churning ocean.

Tom went back to his cabin, and he brought back an half-empty gallon whiskey jug. He took a swig as a salute to the end of Mr. Lemmon's evil reign. "To you, Mr. Lemmon, may you perpetually swab the decks of Davey Jones' ghost ship and may his maggoty whores claw your eyes out." Then, Tom placed the whiskey jug by the rail and he retired.

The captain called the alarm in the morning and the ship was searched for Lemmon. The captain found the whiskey jug, which Tom said was stolen from his cabin. He assumed that Lemmon had met with a drunken accident, then he promptly proceeded to drain the remaining liquid in the jug.

Australia
# Chapter 21

After weeks at sea, Tom's ship finally made it's first port of call - Rio De Janiero. Tom went ashore to stretch his legs, consume some fresh food and inquire about Mirelli's ship. He learned from the harbor chief that his sister's ship had been making better time than his, as they had been there several weeks before.

Mirelli's ship landed in Botany Bay after nearly a year at sea, and she was sent with a group of convicts to serve as laborers on the plantation of Colonel Jonathan Sims, a corrupt ex military man. She was immediately put to work beside the men clearing land upon her arrival to the plantation. In stifling heat, the men chopped down trees, dug up stumps, and milled the lumber into planks. The few woman prisoners were put to work carrying water to the men, cleaning up debris, and stacking lumber. Mirelli was exhausted by the end of the first day, her hands were blistered and full of splinters.

On Mirelli's first night, after she was fed, she was given

a pair of canvas trousers and a rough shirt to replace her dress which had been shredded to rags in her rough environment. Then, she was led to a large shed-like building and locked inside, along with a dozen male convicts and a frail older woman. While she was trying to get herself situated in a livestock stall occupied by herself and the older woman, Mirelli heard rough men's voices. She turned and was startled by a group of wild-eyed men. They forced Mirelli into a corner and threatened to "botanize her."

As they began to rip off her clothing, a thick-necked, scar-faced brute of a man named Kirby forced the men from around Mirelli. He bellowed gutturally, "Get back, you scurvy bastards! This tart's for me! Take old Aunt Mary here if you must cool your passions!"

As Kirby dragged the fighting and kicking Mirelli back to his stall, the pack of human garbage threw the frightened old woman to the ground. A grimy hand muffled her screams as sick humanity frolicked in the night.

Mirelli resisted Kirby's advances, with his meaty hands he beat her until she refused to rise from the straw. Kirby stood before her in his pungent and disgusting nakedness. He told her, "you belong to me from this day forward. If any man touches you, I'll kill him." Then Kirby blew out his candle and proceeded to rob the teenage girl of her virginity in the lice-ridden pile of rags that was his bed.

Tom's ship finally reached Botany Bay after many month's at sea, with the exception of brief stops at the several ports of call to replenish the water and food stocks. The ship anchored in the harbor and several government officials came aboard to make arrangements to accept the prisoners.

Tom's luggage was loaded into a boat, then he and some of the crew were rowed to the docks. Tom was helped with his baggage which was set out of the boat onto a wooden dock. As Tom was thanking the sailors for their help, he was approached by an old weathered Irishman. "Pardon me sor, would you be a needing assistance?"

"Yes, I certainly would. Could you take me to a decent place to rest and get a good meal?"

The Irishman helped Tom with his baggage. "Mrs. O'Reilly's boarding house is a good place to lay yer head and her food is excellent. It's just a short ride away sor."

It was getting late, but there was still enough light for Tom to enjoy the ride as he took in the views of the strange flora and fauna of Australia. He saw several odd birds that he could not identify, even the trees looked strange to him. Tom was surprised to see a very familiar sight off in the distance on the crest of a low hill, it was a Gypsy bender tent. He could see in the low light of dusk that there was a fire over which hung a pot hook and iron pot. "Who lives in that tent up there on the hill?"

The old Irishman craned his neck and squinted his eyes to see what Tom was talking about. "My eyes ain't as sharp as yours, sor. What tent are you talking about?"

"The low one, in the Gypsy camp on the Hill."

"Oh, that ain't no Gypsy camp. That's just Billy Boswell."

"Billy Boswell?"

"He calls himself Billy Bozell. He is quite a character."

"And he's not a Gypsy?"

"No sir, he's a half breed aborigine. That would be a mulato to you Englishmen."

This intrigued Tom. He knew a true Romany outfit when he saw one, unless perhaps it was a *mumper*(tramp) who had been around Gypsies long enough to pick up their style of tent making. "A negro lives in that tent?"

"Yes sor, they calls them Korri fellows around here. That is sort of a tribal name, though they come from several different groups."

"Korri fellows? How interesting."

The Irishman pulled up to a tidy white clapboard establishment with a veranda running across the front and around the sides. "This is it sor, hope you enjoy your stay."

Tom reached into his pocket and from it, he drew two silver shillings. He put them into the eager outreached hand of the Irishman, who seemed surprised at Tom's generosity. "Thank you much, sor. Just ask Mrs. O'Reilly to send for Huey Corrigan if there is anything I can do for you, and I will rush to your service."

"Much oblige, Mr. Corrigan."

"Just call me Huey, if you please, sor."

Tom walked through an open door into Mrs. O'Reilly's. He passed two rough-looking sailors who were sitting at a table, drinking beer. As he passed, they both became silent and stared at the newcomer. "Carry on, gentlemen. Don't let me interrupt your evening."

The men went back to talking and drinking, and Tom walked up to a middle-aged woman who stood behind a small counter. "Hello, madam, Mr. Corrigan highly recommended your establishment to me. Would you have a room available for a tired traveler?"

"I certainly would, sir, and you tell Mr. Corrigan that I am still mad at him. Though, I thank him for touting my house."

Mrs. O'Reilly took Tom upstairs to a small bedroom, with a wash basin and a nice open window overlooking the harbor. "This will do just fine, ma'am. I may be staying a week or so."

Mrs. O'Reilly smiled, seemingly happy for Tom's business. "Sir, if you be hungry, then I can bring you some cold chicken and some ale."

"That I am, and thank you for your kindness." Mrs. O'Reilly left the room and Tom examined the bedding. He was surprised to find that it was clean and freshly washed. As he rested on his bed and waited for his meal, he pondered what the coming day would bring and in what condition he would find Merreli.

Tom awoke early. He retrieved his bag of gold sovereigns which he had hid under the frame of his bed and placed it in his pocket. He opened a thin prayer book and took from it the folded letter from Judge Kingsley which was addressed to the governor of New South Wales. This precious letter was the only thing that stood between his sister's freedom and a life of slavery and misery. Tom was now on a mission and he would bring Mirelli safely home to England whatever the consequences.

Tom walked down the stairs to the dinning room. He greeted Mrs. O'Reilly and took several boiled eggs from her for his breakfast.

"Ma'am, could you please put me in the way of getting Mr. Corrigan to assist me into town?"

"Certainly, I'll have Black Billy take you to him. I'm expecting him to arrive in a short while with a delivery of eggs."

Just then, through the doorway Tom saw the smiling face of a tall thin young black man of about twenty years. The young man approached carrying a net bag filled with several dark, enormous eggs.

Mrs. O'Reilly addressed him. "Billy, you're late. All these Jack Tars had their hearts set on emu egg omelettes. They had to settle on two dozen puny chicken eggs and it cost me a pretty penny."

"Truly sorry, ma'am, but with the drought and all, my suppliers had to walk ten miles to find these few eggs. I did me best."

The young black man took payment for his eggs and then walked outside. As he did so, Tom could see that the diners resented his presence. "Bloody Koori fella, he walked in here like he owns the place. Did you see him? He looked us straight in the eye, like he was the bloody prince of Wales. Someone needs to teach his black ass some manners."

Mrs. O'Reilly took offense and ran up to the mouthy seaman's table. "Why you barnacle-faced bastards. Beside you he is the prince of Wales. I wouldn't be able to feed your gullets without his supplying me with wombat steaks and ostrich eggs. You best not slap the hand that feeds you."

"Yes, ma'am." said one of the diners. But the nasty one gave her a hateful look and he walked out.

"Good riddance! You keep your filthy nibbs out of my place."

Tom followed Black Billy outside and hailed him. "You say your name is Billy and your father is an Englishman?"

"Yes sir, and what's it to ya?"

"There is a possibility that I might know him. That is, if he lived in a tent like yours."

"That is a mighty queer question to be asking sir, unless you also lived in a tent like mine."

"Ha! Bred, born and raised in one - up and down the lanes of England."

"Well then, you best *pen mandy tuttie's nav* (tell me your name), because you be my people."

Tom extends his hand to Billy. "Tom Stanley, son of Adam Stanley the *bora corramengar* (great fighter).

"My father was Miles Boswell, son of Absalom. He was transported here for the term of his natural life for stealing a team of mules. And me dear mother was a poor old aborigine woman. Me dad was worked so hard and beat that he run off into the bush. He took up with me mum's tribe and became a sort of chief. They're both gone now."

"Well, it looks like your dad raised you to be a proper Romnichel *moosh(man)*."

"That he did, sir. He taught me everything he knew, except how to be accepted by the black fellow or the white man. He taught me to be an island onto myself, to be strong even though I am the only one of my kind, a kaula(black)Romnichel."

"Billy, it may make you feel better to know that in England the darker the Romnichel the more pride he has in his blood. He considers himself more *tatchi*(pure) than the other light colored Gypsies who might have a lot of *gauja* blood in them."

"That will be a site to see, Mr. Tom."

"What?"

"When I get to England and put my black arm up against the purest Romanchel's arm and call him a *posh rat*(half blood)."

"Billy, I think that you and I may be in for a few larks if we can get my business settled. Say, I remember something else about your family. Your dad's mum, old Milly Boswell - she was the great *dukkamenger* at Epsom Downs, she *dukkered* the *denla*(crazy) King George, angering him by telling him to avoid war with America. She insisted that he would lose the next war which he entered. He was so upset with her that he paid her with a handful of coppers which he threw on the ground."

"I've heard the same story from me Dad. What might a foot loose and fancy free Romnichel like yourself be doing so far away from your usual haunts."

"My younger sister, Mirelli, was falsely accused and sent here. I've come with release papers to gain her freedom."

"Oh, Mr. Tom, that is not good. There are some very dangerous men in my country. You have to be very careful how you deal with them. They will take every advantage they can of you. But don't worry, I will help you if I can."

"Thank you, Billy. I will keep that in mind. I'm waiting for Mr. Corrigan. He is coming with his wagon to bring me to the governor's office to deliver Mirelli's release papers."

"That old tinker is a sharp one. You tell old Huey that Black Billy told you to keep both hands on your purse when you're around him, and to not buy any false gold rings from him. Keep a straight face, though. And when he gets so worked up that he can hardly hold himself together. Tell him that I was just joshing and that I said that he was as honest as the day is long, because he really is a man of principle. But he does take himself a bit too serious."

"I will do just that Billy, but first I'll need him for my business."

Adam walked down to the main road and waited for old Huey. Huey picked him up and took him to the governor's office. Adam walked into the governor's office with the release paper in hand. He saw a thin bespectacled man sitting at a large desk. He was the Governor's personal secretary.

"I've come to see the governor."

"Sir, the govenor is indisposed, may I help you?"

"I've come from Southamptom with official documents from the chief magistrate ordering the release of my sister who was falsely accused. She was convicted and transported here this spring."

The secretary looked at the document. "Sir, how do I know that this document is official?"

"Why, by the official seal affixed to it, and by the chief magistrate Horatio Kingsley's signature upon it."

"I have no copies of Kingsley's signature with which to compare this document."

"You have no other documents from Kingsley?"

"Not here, but I can send a request to Van Diemans Island offices. They may have one there."

"How long would that take?"

"Some weeks, maybe a month. It all depends on when an official dispatch is ordered."

"That will not do. My young sister is innocent. Each day that she spends at labor, I fear might be her last."

"Sir, if you could see this from my point of view. There have been several hardened criminals released on the basis of forged release papers. It is much easier to forge a release document than it is to counterfeit a pound note. Australia is a penal colony overflowing with swindlers and counterfeiters sent here for doing just that. I'll tell you what I can do. I will write a letter to Colonel Sims explaining your situation. You can present it and your documents to him. I'll leave the release of your sister up to him. He is the man who paid for her transportation and servitude indenture. He is the man who has the most to lose if this document is false."

"Well then, forge me an official note to your lord, mister clerk. If it doesn't work then maybe I can pay your god, Colonel Sims, for his trouble with a currency he understands."

At that moment, Tom emptied his pouch of gold sovereigns and they spilled out onto the clerk's desk.

"Mr. Stanley, we are not barbarians here, we are civilized men. Take your money, since I'm sure you will not need it. And I wish you luck in your endeavor to win the release of your sister."

Tom gave the clerk a look of doubt. "Certainly, I can tell how very concerned you are."

Tom was disappointed at not being given official release papers for Merelli. He thought what a strange land Australia was, where the wealthy landowners had more power than the government officials.

Tom had sent Old Huey on his way after he had dropped him off at the government offices. He wanted to walk and explore and get some exercise to blow off the steam that had been building up inside of him. On his way back to Mrs. O'Reilly's tavern Tom looked up on the hill to see smoke coming from Billy's campfire. So, he decided to pay Billy a visit. As he approached the camp, he smelled the appealing aroma of well-seasoned meat roasting on Billy Boswell's spit. "Hello Billy, what's that joint of meat you got cooking there?"

"It's a bitta kangaroo *hur*(leg). I *moored*(killed)it with my sling this morning. I sold the rest of the meat to Mrs. O'Reilly to feed to her *suv milar(breeding mule-i.e sterile stud) customers.*"

"You said Kangaroo? That's not tatchi Romanus. You meant kanengro(hare)didn't you?"

"No, Mr. Tom, I mean kangaroo. I heard the story from me dad about Captain Cook and the great hare that his men shot and brought back to the ship. One of the men told Cook that the natives called it a kangaroo.

Well, none has ever found a native who knew what that word meant because it was a Romnichel who was with Captain Cook. They supplied the word as a joke and it is now what we all call the animal. At least that is what me dad thought and he had a chance to talk to old aborigine men from many different tribes, nobody knew the word. In fact, some of them used to call the crazy old white men who came to study the aborigines, 'kangaroos,' because it never failed that one of them would hop around and ask them, 'Do you know Kangaroo, Kangaroo?' which of course none understood."

"That is funny, and I do remember hearing some of the old Romnichel men who spoke deep Romanus refer to a hare as a *Kan-guero*, meaning an 'ear fellow.'"

"Yes, exactly. There was an awful lot of our people sent across the water and they are responsible for several other Australian words that came from *Romanus*(Romany language), but the *gaujas* will never *gin*(know)."

"That reminds me, Billy, I was astonished when those low class men at Mrs. O'Reilly's called you a Koori fellow. Can you explain that?"

"My mother's people have different names for their clans and their tribes. There are lots of different tribes who speak different languages, but Koori was never one of their tribal names. But somehow now all of the white people and even the black people call the aborigine men korri fellows and even call the women koori people. I asked my father if he knew from where this word came. My dad said that he and the other Romnichel prisoners always called the aborigine men *Koori*(penis) fellows because thy were always naked and had large manhoods."

"That sounds reasonable, Billy, but what about this big hub bub that I hear about they call a *corra bori*?"

"You mean *corroboree*, the one next week?"

"Yes, what's that all about?"

"It is a time to get together for all of the nearby tribal people. The men have fun showing off their bravery by running at each other and throwing sticks. Sort of like a war game."

"Oh I see, sort or like a Romnichel *bori cora* (big fight), except it's all in fun."

"Yes, I think that some Romnichel language got pidginized here again."

"Well, it looks like the kanengro is burning so you best take care of it. I must hurry and get back to Mrs. O'Reilly's before the *suv milars* eat all of her kangaroo stew."

"You can stay and eat with me, Mr. Tom, there is *dosta(enough)* for the both of us."

"Thank you Billy, but maybe another time. I have to get back and clean up. I have to get me a nice mug of that delicious beer she serves. Squier's is the brand, I believe."

" Yes, it is and Squier's was a *tatchi*(true) Romnichel. He was the first man to brew beer in Australia, but that is another story, Mr. Tom."

"Billy, please call me Tom. We are cousins, you know."

"Okay, cousin."

The next morning, just as was ordered, old Huey arrived with his wagon. "Well, sor, are ye ready for your trip to Colonel Sims?"

"As ready as I can be, and I have my hopes high that all will work out to my advantage."

"Well sor, I will say a little prayer that all the saints be with you in your endeavor to get your little sister back home safe with ye."

"Thank you, Mr. Corrigan, that's good of you."

They head northwest, skirting the Paramatta River

until they came to the Baulkham hills. They took a road that brought them by some lesser land grants where the landowners just had a few convicts to help him farm the land. These land owners generally had good relationships with their laborers and were mostly fair with them. When their terms of service was over, they would give them some property and help them start their new lives with gifts of equipment and household items.

Just as they began to pass into the vast plots of land under the control of Colonel Sims, Huey and Tom saw fields of corn, barley, hops and even tobacco. They passed a cornfield where an armed guard stood watch over a gang of convicts. They were mostly men, but a few half-naked women worked barefoot in the fields, in blistering heat, as they laboriously hoed weeds from between the crop rows.

Huey steered his wagon right up to the Colonel's estate. They were stopped by an overseer as they approached the mansion. "State your business."

Huey spoke up, "We are here to see Colonel Sims on official business."

"Huey Corrigan, since when has an old Irish object like yourself ever been connected with official business?"

"This business is not about me. Mr. Stanley has a letter from the governor's office to deliver to the Colonel."

"Is that so? Then I'll take him to the colonel, but you best stay in your wagon."

The overseer led Tom up to the mansion, and around back where the colonel was holding court with several of his cronies. "Colonel, there is a Mr. Stanley here to see you. He has official papers. He tells me that he has come from England on a mission to rescue a young lady who is in your employ."

"Is that so? Did you tell Mr. Stanley that young ladies

are precious commodities around here?"

"No, colonel, I thought I should leave that to you."

Colonel Sims put on his reading glasses, he took the papers and he quickly scanned them.

"You thought?"

"Mr. Jones, I don't pay you to think. I pay you to do your job and to shut your mouth."

"Yes, Sir."

"Now, about these documents. I don't like the tone of them. The only good thing about them is that the secretary left the matter up to my discretion."

Tom spoke up, "Sir, may I have your answer?"

"Patience, patience, young man. You see, here in Australia a female convict is a very valuable thing - especially a young and comely one. They keep the men happy at their work and offer them a little evening distraction."

Tom became infuriated. "You are dealing with an innocent young woman here! If she comes to harm, I will have my satisfaction from whomever harms her. And if you are responsible, then Sir, you will pay for your mistake."

"Listen, Mr. Stanley. I am unaccustomed to being pushed, and I will push back if need be."

Tom settled down. "Well sir, then what will it take for you to release my sister?"

"This piece of paper is not enough to force me to free your sister. Let's say, if you add fifty guineas to the offer I might consider a deal."

Tom took the pouch of gold coins from his pocket. "I have but thirty guineas."

"Well, I'm a businessman, Mr. Stanley. What else do you have to offer in lieu of the twenty guineas you are short?"

"Sir, I've heard that you are a gambling man and a fan of the boxing sport. I'd like to let you know that I've had a few matches in the ring and I can hold my own. I propose to you that I wager my gold for my sister's freedom. I wager that I can defeat any man Jack among yous! So, if your man bests me, you shall keep the gold and my sister. If I beat your man, then I take my sister and you still keep my gold."

"Well, Stanley, you are a man who talks my language. How could I possibly turn down your challenge - especially since it was overheard by all of these distinguished sporting gentlemen."

Sims friends became excited at the mention of the proposed boxing match. They eyed Tom up and one of the men actually stepped forward and felt Tom's muscular arm.

Sims brushed his friends away from Tom. "Now let him be. Let's not start laying odds on the man just yet."

Tom was relieved now that he knew he had an opportunity to save his sister. He patiently waited for Sims to speak to him. "Stanley, you tell your driver to bring you to Little Bay Beach at ten o'clock Saturday morning. That should give us time to set up the contest. Then we shall see if you can handle your fists as well as you handle your mouth."

Tom handed Colonel Sims his bag of gold coins. Sims held the leather poke in his hand for a moment, as he studied Tom. He seemed in deep thought, then the expression on his face softened to reflect a trace of pity. He opened the poke and drew out five sovereigns which he gave to Tom. "Here, Stanley, I can't take a man's last shilling. Besides, if you can't eat then you can't fight, and you can't get there unless you pay your driver. So, don't think of this as an act of charity."

"I won't, but you are right, and as a man I thank you for giving me this opportunity."

Tom offered his hand to Colonel Sims, who, in return, gave him a firm handshake.

"See you Saturday morning, Stanley, I want you to be at your best."

When Tom got back to Mrs. O'Reilly's he began planning and training for the fight. The next evening Tom ran into Billy Boswell. "Mr. Tom, I heard that you are going to fight Colonel Sims' toughest man."

"Now how would you know that, Billy?"

"Word travels fast around here. One of the colonel's sons was asking around if anyone knew anything about you or your fighting abilities. He came up to my tent and I told him that you could hold your own against any man. He told me to keep quiet and he put a gold coin in me hand. I heard that the colonel's man, Kirby, is favored two to one over you."

"That was smart of you, Billy, because this means that the colonel may be duping his betting friends and putting his money on me. It's always a good sign when your enemy has your back."

"Mr. Tom, I want you to know that me dad trained me to fight in the British ring rules. I'm your man if you need a second."

"Thanks, Billy. I'd be honored to have you."

Tom got up at sunrise Saturday morning and Mrs. O'Reilly served him a breakfast of bacon, Emu eggs, a nice mug of tea and hot soda bread with butter and honey. As he enjoyed his meal, he could see the shadow of someone standing outside of the door. It was Billy who couldn't come in and eat with Tom because of his race. But the aroma had enticed him to stand in the shadows, watching Tom eat. Tom felt guilty and it hurt him that Billy had to be treated like an outcast not fit for white man's society. Tom called Mrs. O'Reilly over. "Ma'am, could you fix up a nice breakfast with lots of bacon and egg on some slices of your buttered soda bread, wrapping it up nicely for me to take along?"

"Why sure, Mr. Stanley. I've got plenty cooked up, since the usual gluttons don't show up this early Saturday morn."

When Tom had finished his meal, he went outside to sit on the veranda and wait for Old Huey. Tom found Billy there waiting for him, and feigned surprise. "Good morning, Billy, you look bright-eyed. Have you had anything to eat?"

"Just some tea and a bita cup of stew left over from yesterday."

"Well then, I'm sure that you have room in your *pur*(belly) for more."

Billy took the food from Tom and he savored every morsel of it. "What lovely food Mrs. O'Reilly has. If I were a *pauna moush*(white man), I would eat here morning, noon, and night."

Old Huey arrived with his wagon. He looked at Billy Boswell and shook his head. "Jehosaphat, Mr. Stanley, what are you doing with this Koori fellow?"

"This Koori fellow is my second and I'd appreciate it if you would call him Mr. Boswell - if you don't mind."

"If I don't mind? Why don't you ask me to call him King Boswell?"

"That is a good moniker for a boxer, Mr. Coorigan. We'll call him King Boswell from here on out."

Billy smiled from ear to ear. He enjoyed seeing old

Huey get worked up. When he got into the back of the wagon he commanded old Huey, "Coachman, his royal highness King Boswell says, 'Drive on.'"

Huey turned to Billy, "Hmph! Royal highness, my rosey red arse."

They arrived on the beach early before Colonel Sims and the sporting crowd. Their only audience was a few boys who were searching for shells along the beach. Tom undressed to the waist and warmed up by running along the shore. He had Billy wrap his hands. Then Billy suggested, "How about a little sparring match with King Boswell?"

Old Huey thought that Billy was just trying to rile him up again, but Billy was sincere. He scratched a line in the sand and posed himself in a proper bare knuckle fighting stance. He and Tom danced and sparred and Tom was very impressed with Billy's style and speed. "Billy, brother, you have the speed and movement of some of the old Romnichel pugilists of generations ago. My dad used to put on a show when he sparred, calling out the names and demonstrating the stances and movements of the great ones that had passed on."

"Mr. Tom, I only know what me dad taught me. Besides the few drunken sailors I have had to tune up, my only other boxing experiences have been with the willing aborigine boys and men of my tribe. Until I beat them so bad that I ran out of opponents."

Tom and Billy continued sparring until Sims and his jovial entourage arrived at the beach. Sims had had his maid servant find clothing for Merelli. She had been brought out of her shed and into the servant's quarters so that she could clean herself up and make herself presentable. This as much for Sims' own sake and reputation as for hers and Toms. Still, he couldn't cover up her haggard look and the scars of hard labor on her hands and arms.

When Tom saw her condition, he was shocked, but he kept his composure. Mirelli was ashamed to look her brother in his eyes. Tom hugged her, "Don't worry, Merelli, you will soon be out of here and back with your own people."

Tom saw Kirby for the first time when he was introduced to him by the referee. Tom looked Kirby over for weaknesses. Immediately he noticed that Kirby had a heavily scarred left eye, which meant that he wouldn't be able to see Tom's right hand punches coming at him very well. He knew that his middleweight physique wouldn't have a chance fighting toe-to-toe with a man of Kirby's brute strength.

The referee laid down the rules of the match and then he scratched a line in the sand. "Alright men, come to scratch." Kirby stood facing Tom with his hands on his hips and he laughed at him. "So, you're the tart's brother. I tell you what. I'm going to beat you as bad as I beat her on our first night together."

Tom didn't take the bait. "She told me that you did beat her up, but you had a problem keeping your flag pole up."

Kirby lunged at Tom and Tom sidestepped, causing him to fall to the ground. When Kirby got to his feet, Tom threw a punch that caught him square on his right eye. Kirby was stunned and blood began to run into his eye, blurring his vision. He came at Tom with flailing arms and he managed to land a punch to Tom's ribs, Tom fell back, holding his left arm against his ribcage to protect it from being hit again. Tom let loose with a strong jab that caught Kirby on his jaw. Kirby was stunned. He fell and was down for a five count.

Tom went at him again when he got up. Billy and Huey were cheering Tom on. "Del his nak(punch his nose), *poger his shira*(break his scull), beat him senseless!"

Old Huey shouted out in his Irish Traveler cant, "carb the yuk in the pi!(punch the man in the mouth!)"

Tom knew that Kirby could hardly see him, so he took the risk to rush in and throw a combination of punches to Kirby's midsection. He threw some damaging shots his stomach and ribs. Kirby now was almost blind from his cut and swollen eyes. He managed to get hold of Tom's left arm and with his mass and strength he dragged Tom out into the water. As he struggled with Tom and pulled Tom out to where he could use him bulk to drown him, Tom continued to beat Kirby's face. Tom got his footing in the sand and he punched Kirby's nose with such force that he broke it. He caused blood to flow back into his nasal cavity. Kirby began to suck in his blood through his nose and spit it out of his mouth, so that he could breathe. Tom took advantage of Kirby's predicament and beat him senseless. Tom then pulled him backwards and held him under the water. Kirby was drowning. Tom held Kirby's head under water until he stopped struggling. Tom looked at his bedraggled sister, then at Colonel Sims who seemed to be enjoying this life-and-death struggle. Tom could see that Sims was surrounded by his sporting friends who by their sober dispositions must have bet on the defeated Kirby. Colonel Sims gave Tom the old gladiatorial signal of thumbs down. "Drown the ox, he isn't worth his salt."

As Tom continued to drown Kirby, Mirelli ran into the water and stopped him.

"No Tom, brother please! Let the man go, he's been punished enough."

Tom dragged Kirby up to the shore and laid him on his side. Kirby soon coughed up water and came to, but he just lay there in total exhaustion.

Tom took Merelli's hand and they walked up to Colonel Sims.

"Congratulations, Stanley. You're more of a man than I thought you were. I'll see to it that your documents are signed and sent to the governor's office. And here, I think that you deserve this for all of that entertainment that you gave us."

Sims handed Tom a bag of gold coins, but this one contained fifty sovereigns.

"This is not my poke."

"I know. I have wronged you and your sister, and besides, you are going to need every bit of that money to live till your sister is well enough to travel and to pay for both of you to have comfortable passages back to England."

Tom waited until Mirelli had recuperated from her ordeal before they began their voyage back to England. They said their farewells to Billy and Mrs. O'Reilly. On the way to their ship, they passed a group of newly arrived convicts who were being held in a roadside corral. Mirelli spotted Janet and Venus, the house maids, among them. "Mr. Corrigan, stop!"

Tom asked, "What's the matter, Mirelli?"

"Nothing, brother. Just sit tight, I see duver juvels(those women) that penned huckabens(told lies)on me."

The well-dressed Mirelli exited her coach and walked up to the fence where the haggard women stared out at her. "Remember me?" Mirelli said. The women weakly smiled and nodded their heads.

One of them spoke, "You're the Gypsy fortune teller, aint you?"

"Yes, that I am. Would you girls like me to tell you about what wonderous things await you in this world?"

Venus and Janet's expressions soured as Mirelli sarcastically continued, "Would yous like me to tell you if you'll soon have a lover? Oh, you'll have many, many lovers. Yes, my dear ladies, and they will all be meatmen."

Mirelli smiled and climbed back into her coach as a guard herded Janet, Venus, and the other prisoners into an open wagon. The guard shouted at the driver, "This load's for Colonel Sims!" Mirelli overheard this and she shouted to the women, "Hey ladies, say hello to Kirby for me." This was a very cathartic moment for Mirelli. She smiled as she hugged her brother Tom and their carriage rolled off towards their waiting ship.

England
# Chapter 22

There was much rejoicing when Tom and Mirelli arrived home. All of their people gathered and threw a great feast for them which included music, food, and drink for all the nearby country people.

Mirelli was happy to be back home with her family. The experience of being transported and abused in Australia had left it's mark on Mirrelli, though she tried hard not to show it. She had drawn close to her mother and had volunteered to work with her at the Fareham mission.

Judge Kingsley had written several letters to Rebecca trying to get her to meet with him, so that he might explain to her why he did what he did. Rebecca just wrote him short, impersonal letters back, telling him to keep his reasons to himself. And that It would be very distressing to Mirelli if he were ever to try to approach her, no matter if it were for an apology. So Kingsley tired of trying to correspond with his daughter, so he decided to go to Fareham and try to talk to her face-to-face.

He arrived at Fareham early one morning. He knocked on the rectory door and he was greeted by Reverend Whitney.

"Mr. Whitney, I have come to ask a favor of you."

"Sir, how may I assist you?"

Kingsley's appearance had changed over the months that followed Mirelli's transportation. He seemed shaky and fragile and very nervous.

"Reverend, If you could contact Rebecca and tell her that I would like to have a personal discussion with her."

"She is at work with the children. If you wait in my study, I will tell her that you are here to see her."

"Thank you, Mr. Whitney. I will wait."

Kingsley sat in the study. Rebecca arrived with Whitney within several minutes, he excused himself to leave her with her father. "Sir, if there is anything that I can do for you or Rebecca, I will be glad to help."

"Thank you, Reverend." Kingsley smiled and nodded to Whitney, then he turned to Rebecca. "Rebecca, I know that I can never make amends with you and my grandaughter. I have been a terrible father to you. But if you give me a chance to explain my behaviour, you maybe can at least understand that I am not an evil person. And though it can never be an excuse for what I have done to you and Merelli, I too have had misfortune and terrible things happen to me in my life. These things have hardened my heart."

"Father, I have only ever heard from you about the great and good things that you have experienced in you life."

"Rebecca, do you remember when as a girl that you always wanted to go on a picnic?"

"Yes I do, and I remember how you reacted in anger

at the mention of the word."

"Well, when you were young, before your dear mother passed away, can you remember when you filled your little easter basket with dainties? You stole a table cloth and sat beneath a tree on the cloth with your dolls. Your dear mother thought it was so cute until you said, 'Mother come picnic with us.'"

"Yes, I do remember that, Father, mother fainted and lay in bed for several days. And you were so severe with me. I remember you crying and holding my arms so hard that you hurt me. And shouting that I was never to say that word again. But I still don't understand the meaning of it all."

"You will, and you must give me one more chance at reconciliation. You are all that I have in this world that means anything to me. The court and my so-called friends all mean nothing now. I will come for you tomorrow morning, you and I will have that picnic that you never had."

The next morning, Kingsley arrived at Rebecca's cottage and Rebecca boarded his wagon. Luckily, Adam and the rest of the family were away at a horse fair, for Adam would have never understood or allowed the despised Kingsley to come near any of his loved ones. Rebecca noticed camp equipment and a large picnic basket in the bed of her father's carriage, but she didn't comment on it.

"Rebecca, I am stopping at Fareham to let Mr. Whitney know that we will be away for a while and for him not to be alarmed. We are going to the Isle of Wight for the picnic."

"Father, why the Isle Of Wight?"

"I have my reasons, daughter. You must bear with me. We must go to The Isle of Wight for this is where our problem started."

Kingsley brought Rebecca to a sailboat that he had chartered with a captain to sail it. They boarded the boat and they disembarked out onto the busy ship lane. Rebecca settled down and tried to enjoy the trip despite the odd feeling she had about the whole thing. Kingsley didn't speak much either. He smoked his pipe and was deep in thought about a time in his life when he young and had no worries.

It was nearly sunset when the sailboat came round a rocky peninsula that jutted out into the blue water of the channel. There against a chalky cliff was a small cove with a beautiful sand beach. Kingsley grabbed the picnic basket and bade Rebecca to board the small dingy which contained the camp equipment. The captain rowed the dingy up to the beach, then, jumped out and dragged it up so that Rebecca and her father could get ashore with dry feet. Rebecca now had an inkling that this beach and a long ago picnic had something to do with her mother's madness and her father's iron will and hard heart, but for the moment she didn't ask him any questions. She knew that whatever had happened would soon be revealed to her.

The sailboat captain unloaded the gear and then he turned to Kingsley. "Sir, when will I know to come and pick you up?"

Kingsley said nothing. He just smiled as he drew a small pistol from his pocket.

"At my signal." He then fired the pistol into the air, startling Rebecca.

"Aye, aye, Sir, understood."

The captain rowed out to the anchored sailboat, and Kingsley walked a short way as he began gathering driftwood for a fire. Rebecca spread a blanket on the sand close to the cliff. She opened the basket and found a piece of bread to stave off her hunger. A nice fire was started and Kingsley served his daughter with the ham, pickles and other delicacies he had brought for the picnic.

"Oh Father, I wish we could have done this when I was a child. After all that has happened, I can honestly say that I am enjoying this special time with you. Everything tastes splendid and I am absolutely famished."

Kingsley smiled broadly, enjoying this rare moment with his beloved daughter. "Rebecca, I too am enjoying this picnic every bit as much as you."

Not an unpleasant word or thought passed between them. They enjoyed a cup of tea and a piece of cake as evening settled in and the fire warmed their faces. The conversation was on happy times. "Father, how did you meet mother?"

"I saw her several times in my youth. I was spellbound by her pretty face, but I was an awkward boy and she never paid me any attention. In my late teens, I got up the courage to ask her to dance. You see, we, she and I, belonged to a group of young people who went to parties, fox hunts and such. Your mother was a golden-haired sylphe. She was the belle of every party and every young man when they saw her would drink in her beauty with their eyes. She would ride in the hunt better than any man. She would bolt to the top of the steepest hill and sit there on her mount and laugh as all of the young men would fall and nearly kill themselves and their horses trying to emulate her feat of daring. I too was one of those foolish young men.

"All of the summer of my twenty first year I pursued her. She bewildered me, and when I thought that I had her in my pocket, she would give an off-handed compliment to one of my handsome friends and lead them on with a wink, just to make me jealous.

"Her father was a commodore. He was a very stern man, and he knew what the goal of most young men was when it came to his beautiful daughter. So we were never allowed to go unchaperoned, not even when she borrowed his sailboat to sail here, to her favorite spot, for a picnic."

"I didn't know that you could sail a boat, father."

"Your mother sailed the boat, just like a professional. She was her father's only child, so he brought her up to know the skills of a sailor and pilot. She knew the waters around here as if she had a map in her head. She and I came here several times in the summer of our engagement. Of course we had a chaperone. It was her father's housekeeper Mildred, who was like a mother to her. But the good thing was that Mildred had a weakness and we were able to bribe her with a bottle of wine. While she would snooze in her chaise, we would walk down the beach or swim out to the sailboat for a little romance."

"Father, thank you for telling me these stories about you and mother. It does mean a lot to me to hear so much about her. I only wish that you would have done this years ago, so that I could have known more about her and what kind of person she was before her problems."

"I felt like the luckiest man in the world the day that she accepted my proposal. You see, I had won the prize in my circle of friends, I had attained the unattainable. The most beautiful and daring woman I had ever seen was going to be my wife. I flaunted it in the faces of all of my doubting friends. We had a beautiful wedding and though I suggested that we go to Edinburgh for our honeymoon, she said that she had a special place picked out for us to go. So, we got ready and packed.

"She took me to her father's sailboat. I was very surprised. She said that now that we were man and wife, she could take me to her beach and do all of the things that she had fantasized about while we were under the gaze of old Mildred the housekeeper. I couldn't argue against that kind of thinking, so we sailed out to our private cove, dropped anchor, and rowed our dingy to the beach.

"For our honeymoon she had brought a small tent, blankets and everything that we would need to spend several days, she even brought fishing poles.

"We put up our tent and started a fire, and we had our evening picnic. We drank a bottle of wine together and kissed until the sun set. Then, we went into our little tent to lay and consumate our marriage. We drank more wine and talked and then we fell asleep. The next thing I heard was your mother screaming. I felt a man's hands on my neck, choking me and I breathed in the foul smell of rotting teeth and rum, as the man continued choking me with his forearm. I tried to fight him off, but he was too strong for me. I was losing consciousness from loss of breath. There was three of them, they were rum smugglers. They had seen the light of our fire and mistook it for their accomplices signal fire. They stoked the campfire until it was burning brightly so that they could examine the beauty of their trophy, your mother. Then, they drug me out of the tent and two of them beat me viciously while a third one held your naked mother before the fire. Then, they tied a rope around my neck and forced me to watch as they tortured and raped your poor mother. I had to watch as two of them at a time attacked her. They bit her and sunk their teeth into her delicate breasts and buttocks. I fought with all of my strength, but then they would choke me until I was unconscious. Then they would slap my face until I revived. One of them taunted me in my hour of distress, 'We don't want the whole loaf mate, just a slice. We'll leave you the rest of the loaf with a few bites took out.' Then they would all howl with laughter.

"I made a painting of those men in my mind so that I would never forget their swarthy faces. And that is why I am such a hard man when it comes to criminals. I see their faces sometimes in the men that I sentence, but until I find these men and extinguish their lives, I will never be at peace with myself."

Rebecca put her hand on her father's shoulder, "Father if I only knew that mother and you went through these terrible tribulations I would have been more understanding, and spent more time with you and tried to help you deal with all your sorrows."

"Daughter you were good to me and caused me little concern, that is all that a father can ask of a daughter."

"What happened then father, how did you escape these men."

"After they had finished their foul deeds with your mother, they sat down and drank our wine and ate the rest of our food. Then they disappeared back into the sea. Some how I got your poor mother back into the sailboat and by some miracle was able to hail some boatmen who were able to get us back to safe harbor. Your mother was taken to an infirmary where her wounds healed but her mind never did. I finished my law studies that year and I vowed to use my knowledge and position to prosecute to the fullest extent any miscreant who came across my docket."

"That is horrible, Father. I can see now why you think like you do, but why do you hate Gypsies so?"

"One of these men was very swarthy and he had his

hair in the fashion of three braids, sidelocks and a pig-tail in the back - like the sailors of the last century. Only Gypsy pugilists continued wearing this style in our era. He spoke in a thieves slang and said a few words which sounded to me like Gypsy."

"Father, Gypsies don't use thieves slang and they only consort with their own people. They don't mix with riff raff. They prefer to interact only with better sorts of people if they associate with our kind."

"Rebecca, I know that I have been wrong about a lot of things. I wished I could have given you a happier child-hood, but that incident changed me into a bitter person. You, on the other hand, have always been kind and chari-table to people. I have been indifferent to the suffering multitudes around me, even though it has given me little happiness in my life. Could you forgive me so that I might salvage what little I have left of my life? I want so much for your's and Mirelli's forgiveness."

Rebecca smiled and hugged her father. He hugged her back, then he looked out towards the sailboat and waved a lantern to draw the captain's attention. After a minute or so, with no reaction from the sailboat, Rebecca spoke."Father, he may be asleep. You were supposed to fire a signal from your pistol."

Kingsley reached into his pocket and pulled out his pistol. "Now Rebecca,cover your ears." He fired his signal shot and shortly thereafter the Captain picked them up from the shore.

Back aboard the sailboat, Rebecca and her father en-joyed each other's company and small talk on their moon-light sail back to Portsmouth.

# Chapter 23

With the countrywide establishment of the Rural Police Force, life became almost unbearable for the English Gypsies. They were hounded from their roadside camps night and day. When they put up the least bit of resistance, they were arrested, jailed, and their property was confiscated to pay their fines.

In the summer of 1854, Adam, Levi, Tom, and their extended family gathered at Marl Pit Oaks. They voted to immigrate to America. August Stankovich decided to return to Romania. He had learned that slavery had been abolished in his country and he wanted to return to bring his people back to England and maybe later America. Laishy decided to stay with his friend Levi.

Stella had lived with Levi as his wife, but she was of such a fiery disposition that she and Levi were always arguing and when Aunt Richanda or Rebecca tried to step in and and settle things, Stella would verbally attack them. When Stella told Levi that she was homesick for her country, and that she wanted to go back to Romania with August's family, Levi protested. But when she admitted to

Levi that when she was a teenager she had had a daughter with the Boyar Mr. Ciobanu and that she wanted to return and try to find her, Levi relinquished and they parted amicably.

So, in the spring of 1854, The Stanleys traveled from Cornwall up the west coast of England. They gathered relatives as they went until a large group of related Romnichel families had gathered in the seaport town of Glasgow, Scotland to prepare for their great exodus from a land that had been their home for centuries.

When Adam and his group reached Glasgow, they went about the business of selling their remaining possessions. They found a ready market for their tents and camp gear in the local Scottish Travelers and a few families of border Romnichels. They had no problem disposing of their horses and wagons by selling them to local liveries and at good prices.

Many of the Adam's people had funds to make the trip to America in first-class but they decided to travel second-class as a survival strategy. They wanted to travel in steerage, below the ship's decks in space formerly used to store cargo. They knew that if they dressed and represented themselves as farmers or common laborers, they would not draw attention to themselves, and besides, how could they explain to the American officials how they came by all of their gold jewelry and collections of silver?

Adam's people possessed considerable wealth in the form of jewelry and gold coins. Now the women went to work mixing yeast and flour to make loaves of bread in which to conceal packets of their prized heirloom jewelry and gold coins. After the loaves were baked, they were placed in baskets to be taken aboard ship - but not eaten. The plan was to deceive the customs officials and it worked.

The other problem was how to conceal the pounds of silver, tea service, plates cups, and silverware that was the pride of each family and also their banking system. One afternoon Levi happened to be watching a barrel maker place a red hot band of metal on a small, wooden barrel that was destined for the whisky distillery across the street. By bribing the head cooper, Levi was able to have him conceal all of their silver in wooden whiskey barrels. Levi brought these to the whiskey distillery and had them filled with Scotch whiskey and labeled for export. These barrels were then taken aboard ship. Adam's people paid the import tax when they reached America, retrieved their whisky barrels, drained them at their leisure and retrieved their treasures.

The Romnichels suffered greatly on the voyage to America, forced into close contact with all manner of people. They were in cramped and stifling quarters, where the hatches were closed at the slightest hint of rough seas, and the sanitary conditions were appalling.

AMERICA
# CHAPTER 24

U pon arrival in New York Adam was met by his cousin Timothy Wharton. Timothy and his wife Hester
had come to America in 1851, to escape her prosecution
for a fortunetelling misadventure. They had been doing
very well and had set up a dukkering camp in a vacant lot
in the city. Timothy told Adam that, since his arrival to
America, he had never wanted for anything. Every week-
end young couples and women would line up at Hester's
tent to have their fortunes told.

Timothy brought the group to a spacious, old hotel
near his camp. The women washed up and went with
Hester on a shopping trip for clothing, the men were con-
tent to sit in the hotel's bar and have a few drinks.

The following days were spent in ordering tents and
having wagons made to order, with specifications from
Timothy who had traveled many roads in this new country.

One day, Timothy took Adam and his sons across the

river into rural New Jersey to visit his favorite stock dealer, an old southern gentleman by the name of Mac Phillips. Mac had come to New York a decade earlier in search of a runaway slave who happened to be his mistress. He never found her, but he fell in love with the city and it's array of beautiful women performing in the music halls. Timothy introduced Adam to Mac and Adam took over from there.

"Mac, I'd like to introduce you to Mr. Adam Stanley. He's in the market for some good horse flesh to pull his wagons."

"Yes, sir, pleased to make your aquaintance. We got some good draft horses and none of them are balkers."

Adam answered, "I see that you do, Mr. Phillips. Say, I just arrived from England and I would like to ask you a few questions about the American horse dealing business."

"It'll be my pleasure, if it makes you happy it'll tickle me to death."

"Very well then, Mr. Phillips, is there much competition in the horse trading business around here?"

"A bit."

"Do you know of any Romany horse traders?"

"Romany horse traders? Mr. Stanley, what do you mean by that?"

"Never mind. What about Gypsy horse traders?"

"Gypsy horse traders? Is there such a thing? Gypsies are from fairy tales. They ain't real people."

"You are exactly right, Mr. Phillips, and don't let anyone tell you different."

# GLOSSARY

## A

**A tatchi moush a tatchi dadus, and a tatchi Rom-nichel - cousta bok and a coushti meripen.:** a real man, a real father and a real Gypsy - good luck and a good life.

**Atrashed:** afraid

**Auva:** yes

## B

**Bal:** hair

**Baulo mass:** pig meat

**Beng:** devil

**Bengler:** devil

**Beshing:** sitting

**Bikoning:** selling

**Bitta lubni:** little whore.

**Bitta moush:** little man

**Boon-tithe:** a gift of food that blesses a person. (English)

**Bora corramengar:** great fighter

**Bora cosh:** big stick

**Bora pani:** great water

**Bori cora:** big fight

**Boyars:** landed gentry. (Romanian)

**Bulls:** butts

# C

**Carb the yuk in the pi.:** Punch the man in the mouth. (Irish Traveler cant)

**Chavies:** children

**Chavies moeys:** children's mouths

**Chavy:** child

**Chi:** daughter

**Chickla bitta chors:** dirty little boys

**Chiv vonger:** put money (in my hand)

**Chor:** boy

**Chored:** stolen

**Choored:** stole

**Chur purri moush:** poor old man

**Churi:** knife

**Corraboree:** Australian Aborigine celebration

**Coushta Jook.:** Good dog.

**Coushta mulo story:** Good Ghost Story

**Coushti:** good

**Cushtiest tattapanni:** best liquor

# D

**Daddus:** dad

**Dawdi:**(exclamation) Lord

**Dear Dawdi:** dear God

**Del his nak:** punch his nose

**Delled:** hit

**Denla:** crazy

**Denlas:** fools

**Dicked:** saw

**Diklo:** A small, leather thong with strings attached to it(chastity belt),or a neck scarf) .

**Divia:** crazy/mad

**Doddle:** feeble

**Dord**i(Dawdi)**, dick duver!:** Lord, would you look at that!

**Dosta:** enough

**Drin:** three

**Dui:** two

**Dui divvus:** two days

**Dukkering juvel:** fortune telling woman

**Duver juvels:** those women

## F

**Foki:** people

## G

**Gauja:** non-Gypsy

**Gauja moush:** Non-Gypsy man

**Gaujafied:** acting like a non-Gypsy

**Gav foki gin:** town officials know

**Gaver:** hide

**Gaver my kucker adre the vesh:** Hide myself in the forest.

**Gavers:** officials

**Gin:** know

**Gry:** horse

## H

**Hatch a tan:** pitch a tent

**Hobben:** food

**Huckabens:** lies

**Hur:** leg

## I

**Inca patru va rog:** Four more, please. (Romanian)

# J

**Jal adre the vesh:** Go into the woods.

**Jall:** go

**Jinned:** knew

**Juckal:** dog. *Plural:* juckals

**Juvals:** women

# K

**Kair:** house

**Kala:** black

**Kanengro:** hare

**Kan-guero:** ear fellow, Figurative name for a hare.

**Kaula moush:** black man

**Kaula Romnichel:** Black English Gypsy

**Kauva kuver's cushty:** This stuff's good.

**Kekker: no, don't,** haven't

**Kekker chor:** No, boy.

**Kerring:** doing

**Koori:** prick/penis

**Koppers:** blankets

**Koushta bok!:** Good luck!

**Kucker:** self

# L

**Latcho! Latcho!:** Good! Good!

**Lel:** get

**Lel a juvel:** get a woman

**Lelled rummered:** got married

**Levinor:** beer

# M

**Mamaliga:** corn meal mush. (Romanian)

**Mandy's kucker:** myself

**Maukidiness:** impurity

**Mauta gauja juvel:** drunk non-Gypsy women

**Mesala:** table

**Minge:** vagina

**Mockerdy:** ritually impure

**Moor:** kill. *Past tense:* moored (killed

**Moosh:** man

**Moushes:** men

**Muey:** face

**Mulo:** ghost

**Mumper:** beggar/tramp.(English)

**Munging:** begging

**Muscars:** policemen/constables

**Muter:** pee

# N

**Naflo:** sick.

**Nashado gairo:** the hangman( from nasher:to choke)

## O

**Opre the drum:** upon the road

## P

**Pange:** five

**Pani:** water

**Paraka tu mirro phral:** Thank you, my brother.(Romanian Romany)

**Pauna moush:** white man

**Pen mandy tuttie's nav:** Tell me your name

**Poger his shira:** break his scull

**Pooker:** tell

**Posh rat:** half-breed

**Pur:** belly

## R

**Racklys:** girls

**Rokker:** talk

**Romnichel:** an English Gypsy

## R

**Rummering:** marriage

## S

**Sar shan, sos me chavis kerring ta rati?:** Hello, how are my children doing tonight?

**Shoshoi:** rabbits

**Shira:** head, forehead

**Shoon, shoon. Kekker pen duver chavy:** Quiet, quiet. Don't say that, child.

**Small holders:** The squatters who had earned the right to live in the forest and let their branded livestock roam its confines.

**So'd ya ker:** What'd ya do?

**So's tutties nav?:** What is your name?

**Star:** four

**Stariben:** prison

**Suv milar:** breeding mule/sterile stud, useless person

**Suv these gaujas:** frig these non-Gypsies

**Suving muscar:** frigging constable

## T

**Tatchi:** true

**Tattipani:** liquor

**Trashered:** afraid

**Tsigan:** Gypsy. (East European)

# V

**Vardo:** living wagon

**Vasavo dik:** bad look

**Vel! Akai, jook!:** Come here, dog!

**Vel! Vel akai!:** Come! Come here!

**Vongar:** money

# Y

**Yek:** one

# Z

**Zlatari:** gold-washing Gypsies